Scorched By Flames

Hidden Realms of Silver Lake
Book 10

Vella Day

Dedication

A big thank you to Zulema Barbosa for inviting us to our first Costa Rica party. You always made us feel so welcome!!

And to Tamarella Higden and her daughter Aislyn for being such gracious hosts in Houston.

The assignment? Kill or be killed. The problem? This she-dragon's target is her destined mate.

Dragon shifter, Zulema Garcia, has been trained as a fierce fighter from an early age. All is well until the day she's captured by the Zon, a group of powerful warlocks and witches. Their demand? To keep her family safe, Zulema must kill Bevon Forrester—a powerful Fey. Zulema is willing to do it—until she realizes Bevon is her one and only mate. Now what is she supposed to do?

Bevon is thrilled that his older brother is next in line to become the Feyrion king, since freely roaming both Tarradon and Feyrion suits Bevon just fine. Only a broken heart could dampen his spirits.

Life is great until an assassin shows up—in the form of a sexy, female dragon shifter. Oh, this should be fun. He can't be killed by the usual methods, so Bevon decides to have some fun with Zulema Garcia.

Let the games begin!

Chapter One

PAIN STABBED THE back of Zulema Garcia's head, throbbing and pulsating until the agony was enough to rouse her into consciousness. Moaning, she licked her dry lips.

What the hell just happened? And where was she? Wherever it was, the stench of this place made her stomach revolt. As bile raced up her throat, Zulema managed to open her eyes and spit out what was left of her last meal.

Like the trained warrior she was though, she assessed her situation to determine any present dangers. When she detected no immediate threats, she worked on a plan to get out of there—wherever that was.

It was dark. That much was evident. And damp, which implied her captor was probably holding her in some kind of basement or underground bunker. What was worse than the fetid smell was the fact that her hands and feet were shackled and bolted to the floor. Crap. Someone was determined to keep her there.

Zulema had been in worse situations—trained for stuff like this in fact—but that didn't mean it would be easy to escape. Thankfully, she wasn't an ordinary dragon shifter. Her father had been a powerful warlock, and as such, she could teleport, among other things.

Closing her eyes, Zulema pictured her home at the edge of Avonbelle Province. With a nod, she imagined flying across Tarradon. When she opened her lids, she hadn't moved. And that made her mad.

"Hey! Anyone there?" she called, unable to keep her anger in check any longer.

This had to have been some kind of mistaken identity. Last night, Zulema had gone out with friends to a local bar. Sure, she'd had a few drinks, but as a dragon shifter, it was near to impossible for her to get any kind of buzz. She remembered leaving through the back of the bar to the alley, ready to teleport home. Only she didn't remember reaching her destination. Or should she say, it was apparent from her current situation that she never made it there. But who would kidnap her? Her family was poor, which meant this wouldn't be about any ransom.

The door to her enclosed room opened, letting in scant streams of light. "I see you're awake. That's unfortunate."

Unfortunate? What did that mean? The man, whose face she couldn't make out, bent over, and unlocked her chains, and a trickle of hoped surged. "Why did you take me?"

"To save you and your family, Zulema."

Damn it. If he knew her name, she'd specifically been targeted, but it still made no sense. "We don't need saving."

He smiled, or at least some light flashed off his teeth enough to make it look like he had. "You do. From us."

Us? Her stomach churned. If she understood her situation better, she would have changed her hands into fire shooting weapons and burnt him to death.

The man bent over her. She felt a prick on her neck, and then her vision turned white.

When she awoke, she was in a different room, one that was a lot brighter and possessed a bed. While this was an improvement, the absolute silence disturbed her soul. What kind of game were they playing?

This room, while cleaner, was too warm. As a dragon shifter, the muggy heat didn't settle well with her, but she'd deal. Because she wasn't tied down this time, Zulema sat up and slowly eased to her feet. The ten by ten room had white-washed cement walls and no windows. There was a toilet attached to the wall and a slightly stained sink with a mirror above it on the other side. This was definitely a jail cell of some kind.

Zulema checked out the room thoroughly, looking for some kind of camera or listening device. When she was convinced she wasn't being watched, she pounded on the door. "Why am I here?"

When no one answered, she returned to the bed. Without a doubt, someone had drugged her. Now that she was feeling a bit better, she concentrated on teleporting the hell out of there. But no matter how hard she tried, she remained in the room, and that fact scared her more than anything. Had her captor somehow stolen her magic? While no one had taken it from her before, she had heard there were people with that ability.

Teleporting wasn't her only skill though. Zulema held out her arms to transform them into fire shooting claws. When nothing appeared, her pulse skyrocketed. She rushed up to the door and pounded on it again. "I want answers."

Then she waited. And waited some more. She paced, but time didn't pass any faster.

Eventually, she decided that the only way to regain her abilities was to rest. The drugs, or maybe it was some spell, would eventually wear off—or so she hoped. They'd also have to feed her, and when they did, she'd make her move.

Zulema returned to the hard bed and lay down and almost instantly succumbed to sleep.

"Wake up," a sharp voice said, his stinking breath close to her face.

He then stabbed her side with some kind of electric poker, forcing Zulema to bolt upright. A man with black eyes and greasy, long hair yanked her to her feet. "The boss wants to talk to you. Try anything and you'll die."

It took some effort not to laugh at his corny line. "Sure. Unhand me, and I'll be a model prisoner."

He jerked her arm at her snarky response. Two other men stepped into the room—dragon shifters to be precise. Darn. With the ceiling only ten feet tall, she wouldn't be able to shift and fight, though at the moment, she wasn't sure she could shift. None of her powers seemed to be working.

Wanting them to believe she had no intention of escaping, she followed the first man. The second and third fell into place next to her. Surrounded. Damn.

The hallway had the same white-washed cement block walls with the same fluorescent lights rimming the ceiling. "Are we underground?" she asked, not really expecting them to answer.

"Yes."

She appreciated the information, but knowing it wouldn't make escaping any easier. Zulema was eventually led to a closed door, and the man who'd awoken her, knocked.

"Come in," said a voice from the inside.

Her guard opened it up and shoved her in. What was up with these people? Whatever. At least, she was still on her feet and no longer in chains.

The office was surprisingly opulent—at least by her standards. Filled bookcases, a lavish gold brocade sofa, and a bar with a vast amount of liquor that took up most of the room. That, and a large man.

"Have a seat," the stranger said.

She blinked a few times, but his face appeared blurred out—which was impossible, unless he was a hologram or some kind of artificial intelligence.

"Are you in this room?" she asked.

"No, which means harming me is impossible."

Darn. Wanting to hear what this extremely life-like image had to say, she sat on the edge of the sofa. Because she was dirty, Zulema didn't want to mess up the furniture and chance being punished.

"Drink?" he asked, as he stepped over to the bar and poured himself a glass of some amber colored liquid. How was that possible if he wasn't there?

"No, thank you."

"It's not drugged."

She lifted her chin. "Do people often accuse you of drugging them?" Someone had given her something to knock her out the first time.

He might have smiled, but she couldn't tell. "Sometimes, but I don't want you harmed. I have a proposition for you."

This ought to be good. "Do I have a choice whether to accept or not?"

"You always have a choice."

That interested her. "Do tell."

"Let me apologize for the way we had to meet."

"You mean from the way you kidnapped, drugged, and restrained me?" she asked, unable to keep the ire from her tone.

"Yes. You see, I need your help."

"Seriously? My help? Just so you know, asking outright, without the kidnapping part, would have been more effective."

"When you hear what I want, you might see why I had to take such drastic measures."

She was tired of this run around. "Just tell me."

"I need someone killed—someone who murdered my mate—and you are the perfect person to do it."

Zulema almost laughed. "For starters, I'm not an assassin." The man had to be on drugs.

"I beg to differ. Haven't you been training to fight your whole life?"

Zulema's blood ran cold. "You've been watching me?"

"Let's say, we keep tabs on those who interest us."

Her skin crawled. "Who are you people?"

"We call ourselves the Zon. We are a cabal of warlocks and witches, here to help restore order to the realm."

Not likely. They probably wanted to destroy all things good. "I'm not interested. Nor would I be any good. I've only killed to protect myself, my family, or a client."

The stranger downed his drink and set it on the bar—a bar that was slightly different from the one in this room. "You don't understand. I know your ill mother and sister are very important to you since your father was tragically killed when you were young."

Breathing suddenly became difficult. At the mention of her mom and sister, every protective gene flared. "They are important but leave them out of this."

Her mother was afflicted with a disease no one seemed able to identify, and she was very near the end of her life.

"On the contrary. We plan to use them to make you do our bidding."

More bile rose up her throat. This was her worse nightmare. "What exactly do you want from me?"

"Just what I said. To kill a man."

"Who?"

"His name is Bevon Forrester, and he murdered my mate. For that, he needs to die."

"If this is about retribution, why not kill him yourself? I bet you'd feel better if you did."

He faced her—or rather his image turned toward her. "That's where you come in. I don't have the ability to do so. You see, the man is a Fey."

Against her will, Zulema laughed. "You do realize Feys can't die?"

"That's what they want you to believe. For one thing, treniam, a special plant, can seriously harm them. I believe that is what killed my mate—that and her fatal wounds."

"I've never heard of that plant."

"It grows only on Feyrion, which is the realm where most of the Feys reside. A number of the plants were harvested here by some demons a while back, but the Feys destroyed the stash. We failed to gather some for ourselves, and that was an oversight on our part."

Now Zulema leaned back against the sofa, not caring if she dirtied it. "Feyrion, you say. No problem. I'll just pop on over there, grab a handful, and ask this Bevon dude to eat some."

The man's expression remained blurred, but from his fisted hands, he didn't appreciate her sarcasm. "One merely needs to touch Forrester's skin with it to weaken him dramatically. Once he is ill, I believe an arrow to the heart would end his life."

So that was why she'd been selected. She was an expert marksman, and the crossbow was her specialty. "Sure. Easy." Or not. "As soon as he notices the arrow heading toward him, he'll teleport. He is a Fey after all." Not that she knew much about his kind other than a few tidbits the witch world had regaled her with.

"He can, but so can you."

Zulema laughed. "Really? Trust me, I can't. I've tried."

"We have blocked all of your powers for the time being. Once you agree to help us, your powers will be restored."

The whole idea that someone could block her powers scared her almost as much as their threat to harm her family—and most likely her. "Even with my powers at full force, I can't create a portal."

"I've solved that problem. Inside the folder in front of you is a small medallion. This will allow you access to Feyrion. I've written down the instructions on how to use the device."

He was something else. "Once I arrive, I imagine there will be sentries to challenge why I am there. It's not like I can tell them that I want to collect some treniam so I can kill Bevon Forrester."

"No. Tell them you are a friend of my late mate's."

He had thought this through. "If I'm a friend of hers, people would expect me to know your name."

The silence that followed spoke volumes—as did the blurred out face. "Fine. My name is Derrick Valoric."

"Thank you. Should I need to contact you about anything, how can I reach you?"

"The same medallion can communicate with me."

She was impressed with his thoroughness, albeit disgusted with the concept of killing anyone in cold blood, whether he deserved it or not. "What can you tell me about this *murderer*?"

Zulema would do anything to keep her family from harm. Considering her mother was helpless in a nursing home, this man and his kind could reach her rather easily—and that thought sickened her.

"There's a dossier in the folder. Study it."

Zulema picked it up. When she opened it, her heart rate sky-rocketed. While she'd never seen this Fey before, Bevon Forrester's eyes were kind. And that smile. Oh, my. That smile made her heart flutter—something that never happened. Though that might have been how he was able to get close to the woman he supposedly killed.

Zulema read further. "Tamarella Warnom was his cousin? Why would he kill her?"

"Why, indeed?" the man asked.

This didn't make sense. "Are you sure he killed her?"

"According to the man my mate was arranged to marry, it was Bevon who killed her."

She held up her hand. "Whoa. I thought you said that this Tamarella woman was your fated mate."

"She was, only her father decided that if she, a Fey princess, married this warlock, that the resulting empires would grow immensely strong."

Arranged marriages didn't happen on Tarradon, though Zulema had heard they occurred a long, long time ago on Earth. "I see. My only job then is to kill Bevon?"

"Yes."

"How do I prove to you that he is really dead?"

"I'll know. The Zon is everywhere." With that the man disappeared.

Zulema expected the doors to burst open and the guards to drag her back to her cell, but no one came. Since she could use that offered drink right about now, Zulema stepped over to the bar and poured herself one. With some hesitation, she sipped the liquid. The warm, smooth liquor was perfect. Not that she had a built-in poison detector in her body, but this was the good stuff.

In case the man returned and asked for her answer, she studied the folder a bit more. It was interesting to note that this Bevon

Forrester had a Fey brother named Kenton who was mated to Tory Sinclair. The Sinclairs were well-known in the realm, and that knowledge might come in handy.

Chapter Two

"**M**OM, I'M GOING to be out of town for a while," Zulema explained to her mother whose lifeless body just lay there. From the way her breathing was shallow, her mom's health was clearly failing. "Can you hear me?"

She'd been sick for so long that Zulema was beginning to forget the mother who had been a fierce and vibrant woman. Zulema had promised herself that she would figure out a way to help her get well. She had to.

Zulema had been released from that terrible jail only a few hours ago—but not before she signed a paper stating that she would make sure that Tamarella's killer would be dead within two weeks. And just like that, she found herself teleporting home with her powers restored. After she cleaned up and packed, she headed to the facility where her mom was being treated.

While she wasn't the type to take anything for granted, losing something as valuable as her ability to shift or to teleport made her appreciate her skills all the more.

Her mother opened her eyes and lifted her hand. Zulema grabbed it. "Where did you say you are…" Her voice faded.

"Going? I have an out of town job. But don't worry. Everything will be okay. I won't be gone long."

Zulema hated lying to her, but the truth would only make things worse. There was no way she'd tell her mom there was some impending danger lurking. It would cause her too much anxiety.

"Okay, sweetheart. Have a good time." Her voice faded.

Just as Zulema was about to let her mom rest, her sister, Maylora, rushed in. "Zulema!" Her sister came over and hugged her. "I didn't expect you today."

"I know, but I had to see Mom. Let's talk in the hall." It would be impossible to explain to her sister why she had to leave the area, but Zulema had to say something. If Zulema told her the real reason for her trip across the province, Maylora would break down. It was understandable since her sister's biggest fear was having men invade her home and brutally kill her—like they had with their father.

"What is it? You look worried," Maylora said.

"I am. A bit. I have a job I have to do, and while I'm gone, I need you to watch Mother."

"Of course, but what is this job? Is it dangerous?"

Zulema usually served as a bodyguard for important female figures. Even though the criminals were equally vicious against men as well as women, too often the men she protected were condescending or too forward. Zulema preferred women for that reason.

"I don't think so, but I need to go to the middle of the province."

"Do you have to?" Maylora asked, worry coloring her tone.

"I do, but I'll be back soon."

Before she gave into Maylora's pleadings, Zulema left. According to the dossier on this Bevon fellow, he resided in the middle of the forest next to the eternal flame. While she'd read about it in books, she'd never visited the place. Zulema had always been too busy learning to fight to study history.

Because she had two weeks to complete the assignment, she couldn't afford to waste any time. Her first goal would be to watch Bevon Forrester in order to create her plan. Then at some point, she'd have to go to Feyrion to retrieve the plant that would weaken this Fey. While the dossier contained a photo of the treniam plant, a realm was a big place. If the plant was poisonous to them, she doubted it would be growing in many places.

As much as she wanted to turn around and demand that Derrick Valoric do the deed himself, he seemed convinced only she could do the job. In the end, she decided to do this or die trying—anything to protect her family.

The closest big city to the forest was Edendale, the capital of Avonbelle Province. Since Zulema would need a place to stay when she wasn't hunting Bevon, she found a hotel room in town. Because of the generous stipend from the Zon, she chose one nicer than what she normally would have stayed in.

Once she checked in, Zulema teleported to the forest, close to the flame. She could have cloaked herself, but what if Bevon happened to be there? While she wasn't the type to seduce a man, her family's life was on the line.

She appeared a few hundred feet from the flame. Without her weapons—other than a few hunting knives she always carried—she sauntered down the forest path toward her destination. Sure, there was a large cement bowl rimmed with fire, but it wasn't as grand as she'd thought it would be for a national treasure. Off to the side was a fountain of some kind. A few pipes were sticking out from the rock face with water pouring out into a small, cement pool. Interesting, but not particularly impressive.

Zulema looked around but saw no one. She doubted the Zon would have misled her. The dossier said that Bevon and his brother, Kenton, were portal sentries. While there appeared to be no portal anywhere, she suspected the men would be close by. It was possible they lived in Edendale and only teleported here to guard the gates to Feyrion during certain hours.

There was a path leading away from the eternal flame, which might be a good place to start her search. Zulema walked west, enjoying how the sun spiked through the leaves, creating a magical setting. A few times she swore she saw bright lights zip back and forth across the path, but they were moving so fast, she wasn't able to tell what they were.

No homes appeared, however. After walking about fifteen minutes, Zulema was about to turn around when a woman popped out from behind a large tree.

"Hello," she said and then smiled. The blonde woman with the heart-shaped face was very tiny—a Fairy perhaps? While Zulema had never met one, the woman might be Fey.

"Hi."

The woman held out her hand. "I'm Fay Forrester."

Zulema's heart dropped to her stomach. Fay was Bevon's sister—at least according to the dossier. "Zulema. Nice to meet you. Are you here to enjoy the amazing day?" She wasn't the best at making small talk. Most of the time, her job required her to remain silent, but this woman could provide valuable information about Bevon's whereabouts.

Her eyes sparkled—literally. "Walk back to the eternal flame with me. We need to talk."

"Have we met before?" Zulema was sure to have remembered this diminutive woman.

"I don't believe so, but I can sense something is troubling you."

Oh, shit. "Are you an empath?"

"Among many things. How is your mother?"

Zulema stopped in her path and spun to face Bevon's sister. No way she was Zon. "How do you know about her?"

Fay placed a hand on Zulema's arm. As much as she wanted to pull away, she couldn't. It was as if the woman was exerting some kind of force field on her.

"I sense your concern, that's all. Perhaps you should take a look at the flame. Or better yet, make a wish in the fountain. I hear wishes often come true."

"I will." Or not. Zulema didn't believe in superstition. They chatted for the next few minutes, but Zulema didn't find the opening to discuss her brother. "Do you live around here?"

She smiled. "I do."

And just like that the woman disintegrated—if that was the right word—into points of light and then dispersed.

"WE HAVE A problem," Fay said, appearing in Bevon's living room without warning.

Bevon dropped his feet to the floor and sat up. "What kind of problem?"

"I ran into a woman who has an agenda."

His sister never was one to speak outright. He swore she loved to tease him. "What kind of *agenda*?"

"She's troubled."

More nonsense. "Come out with it, wench!"

She laughed. "Your trips to those medieval festivals in Edendale have to stop."

He laughed. "I'm impressed you even know where the word comes from."

"Earth spawned the great bard, Shakespeare. He used the term to mean a lovely young lady. While I am anything but young, I'll take it as a compliment."

His sister didn't look a day past thirty. It was the benefit of being more or less immortal. "Should I be worried about this woman?" Bevon was enjoying the troubled look on her face.

"Yes."

"Is she out to kill me?" Not that she could.

"I don't know."

Bevon stood, traipsed over to the kitchen, and retrieved a beer. "Want one?"

"No, thank you."

Since he wasn't busy at the moment, he would continue chatting. He always did love a new conspiracy theory. "What is this woman's name? Surely, you learned that much."

"Zulema."

"Interesting name. If I recall my history lessons, it means peace and tranquility."

"Yes, but this woman was not at peace," Fay said, her chin notching up a bit.

He twisted off the bottle cap and tossed back a good portion of his beer. "What's going on, Fay? You usually don't believe we are in harm's way." He waved a hand. "Sure, Kenton was attacked by those demons, but…" That thought concerned him. "Don't tell me this woman is a one of them?"

"Hardly. A dragon shifter to be precise, but I think she means to harm you. I could sense her inner turmoil. Her mother is ill."

His sister still wasn't making any sense. "What role do I play? I don't even know her or her mother."

"I don't know, but I believe it won't be the last we see of her."

That rather interested him, or else he was just bored. "What does she look like?"

Fay wagged a finger at him. "Always interested in a woman's looks. You need to dig deeper, brother. See into her soul."

Once more, Bevon laughed. "Are you implying I'm shallow?" That was probably true. He loved women and women loved him.

It wasn't his fault that his older brother was the unlucky bastard who had to inherit the king's throne when the time came.

"Someday you'll find your mate, and then you won't know what to do."

"Ouch." True or not, he wasn't ready to discuss that aspect of his life. "You never answered me about what this troubled girl, who is out to get me, looks like."

"Fine. She's tall—though everyone is tall compared to me. I'd guess five-feet eight. Built well with long, straight, black hair. She's not just a dragon shifter. She can teleport."

His body tingled at that combination. "She's not of Fey descent, is she?"

"No. I'm thinking witch."

"I can handle that. Humans are such vulnerable creatures." And loving ones, too.

Fay shook her head. "There you go again. Dismissing her. I'm just saying—be careful around that one." With that, Fay disappeared.

Darn. He should have asked where this mystery woman was

from. His sister seemed to have extracted quite a bit of information from her. Many people passed through the area to see the immortal flame, since it was a realm treasure, and yet Fay rarely spoke to any of them.

"Is this woman still around," he telepathed his sister.

"No."

He waited for Fay to offer up more information, but she did not. Something was up with her, but he had no idea what. *"Do you know where she lives?"*

"She's staying in Edendale. That's all I know."

"Thank you."

That entire encounter was rather strange. There was something his sister wasn't telling him, but it didn't matter. How hard would it be to find a raven-haired beauty who was a blend of dragon shifter and witch? To say the least, Bevon loved the challenge of trying to find her.

It might be a good time to drop in on his brother and his mate and have a chat. One of them might have heard about a threat to the Feys.

When Kenton and Tory had first gotten together, they mostly stayed in Edendale, because Tory worked in town. As her teleporting skills improved though, she agreed to live in the woods part of the time.

"Hey, brother. You free?" he telepathed.

"Kind of...busy...here."

Bevon understood what that meant. Oh, well. A trip into town always did wonders for his soul anyway.

Chapter Three

ZULEMA HADN'T LEARNED much from Bevon's sister. Fay Forrester seemed nice, but her ability to almost read Zulema's mind was a little creepy. Even though she'd been trained to steel her mind against intrusion, this woman apparently could see right through her. Killing Bevon Forrester might be harder than Zulema thought.

After following Fay's suggestion of returning to the eternal flame, Zulema took the time to read the plaque on the stone bowl. She had to admit, staring into the flames was mesmerizing and centering, though not as transformational as she'd hoped. No oracle appeared to tell her how to proceed with the mission. Even without any divine answers, she was quite certain that if she didn't kill Bevon Forrester, her mother and sister would die.

Despite being a non-believer in anything fanciful, in case there was anything to this make-a-wish-at-the-fountain thing, Zulema stood in front of the pooling water and prayed that her mother would soon receive the help she needed.

Before she was ready to leave, a couple arrived at the flame. Wanting to give them some privacy, Zulema left. While she could teleport to town, she needed time to think, and flying always boosted her endorphins and would hopefully provide her with a clearer mind.

When she landed on the outskirts of the city, Zulema chose to walk the rest of the way to her hotel. If she was going to be in Edendale for close to two weeks, she wanted to take the opportunity to see what this city had to offer. She came from a small town, and while pretty, Zulema had always been attracted to the hustle and bustle of a larger town.

Before she took the time to explore any stores though, she needed to figure out the next move for her assignment. That meant memorizing everything that was in the dossier.

After returning to her hotel room, Zulema went to work, making a list of the people who might have been involved in the death of Tamarella Warnom. Obviously, she had to put Bevon Forrester at the top, but she wanted to be thorough. Judging him without facts wasn't her style.

After reading everything Derrick Valoric provided her a few times, it became clear that the only chance she had of killing Bevon was if he became weak from exposure to treniam. And that meant procuring the plant from Feyrion.

There was one issue with that. Even if she succeeded in creating the portal to the other realm, she'd need to convince the sentries on the other side that she was indeed a friend of the fallen woman. But how? Zulema read through the dossier one more time. Only at the end did it say Tamarella was killed anywhere from one week to ten days ago. Why didn't Derrick Valoric know the exact date? Was it possible he had been blocked from entering Feyrion, and this information was given to him by another source—one who wasn't able to reach anyone in Tarradon in a timely fashion?

It didn't really matter. Zulema would use the information she'd been given. Because Valoric apparently loved Tamarella, he was aware of every cousin and major player in his mate's life. All were listed in a fair amount of detail. Some were even accompanied by a photo—most likely provided by his mate.

After several hours of last minute studying, Zulema felt confident that she could pull it off saying that she was Tamarella's friend. The Fey woman's friend loved to design jewelry as a hobby. Because Zulema didn't have time to take any classes on this topic, she wanted to at least have a working knowledge of such things. It was probably for the best that Tamarella wasn't around to spot Zulema as a fake.

Tomorrow would be a good time to make her move. For now,

she'd do a little jewelry making research.

By nine that night, Zulema's eyes were practically crossing. As much as she tried to concentrate, she couldn't. In need of food, she went downstairs to the front desk to ask about the location of a casual bar, one suited for a dragon shifter. The manager was a shifter himself and probably knew of some good places.

"I suggest Wings. It's low key, classy, and has great food. Best yet, it's within walking distance, though they do have a landing pad on top of the building should anyone need to take flight."

"Thank you. I'll walk."

After the manager drew her a map, Zulema left, and to her delight, the fresh air revived her. Since sleep was probably off the table for many hours, she needed to clear her head before taking one last stab at learning the ins and outs of the Forrester and Warnom families.

The Wings Bar was easy to find, and the interior was what she expected from a big city. Wood paneled walls, scarred floors, and tables and booths crammed in the middle that created an intimate atmosphere. A long bar sat along the side, and in the back was a small dance floor. It screamed casual but friendly, exactly what she was hoping for, and the number of shifters made the air rich with testosterone. Because of her witch heritage, Zulema could sense almost every kind of entity—a talent that had served her well.

A pretty waitress seated her in a booth across from the bar, giving her the chance to study everyone—something she found enjoyable and relaxing.

She ordered immediately, and the food was delivered quickly. Zulema sipped her drink, while working hard not to scarf down her delicious meal. The desk clerk had been right. This was a good place.

She was almost finished with her meal when every cell in her body tingled. When Zulema looked up, her heart stopped. It was Bevon Forrester in the flesh, and she had to literally remind herself to breathe and then to swallow.

He glanced over at her, but then turned around and headed to the bar. It was almost as if she had been invisible. Not that he would have any idea who she was, but Zulema didn't trust that his sister hadn't mentioned or described seeing the troubled woman she'd met near the flames. Thankfully, Zulema hadn't mentioned Bevon's name to Fay, so his sister would have no reason to tell him.

As much as Zulema wanted to study the man, she feared he might sense her staring. That was crazy, but stranger things had happened.

Bevon slipped onto a stool, and the bartender came over to greet him. From the way he smiled, he and Bevon were acquaintances. A woman sat down next to Bevon, but he didn't turn his head. From that response, they weren't together. Zulema wasn't sure why that pleased her, other than the fact there would be one less person to mourn him when he died.

Not wanting people to notice her watching Bevon, she waved to her server for her check. Once she paid, she waited until Bevon was deep in conversation with the bartender before leaving.

Sad to say, her heart didn't stop pounding until she'd returned to the hotel. Zulema was rather disgusted with herself for her reaction to the man. She was a warrior, trained not to react to the presence of the enemy. But this Bevon Forrester altered something inside her, and she didn't like it. Not one bit.

THE MOMENT BEVON entered Wings Bar, he sensed something was different. The bar was…more electric than usual. Highly sensual. And very stirring. He immediately looked around to find the source.

The moment he set eyes on the raven-haired beauty, his pulse soared, and his cock hardened. Not wanting to stare and catch her attention, he memorized her face and then turned to Finn McKinnon, the man mated to Tory's twin sister.

That must be the mysterious Zulema that Fay had warned him about. The woman couldn't have known he'd be there tonight. In fact, had his brother been free, Bevon would be enjoying a drink with him at Kenton's mate's house right now.

Bevon slid onto a bar stool, trying to look unaffected by the sexy siren. She was what Fay was worried about? She was but a slip of a thing.

"Bevon," Finn said. "What can I get you?"

"A beer." He leaned forward. "See that woman in the third booth on your left?"

"The pretty siren with the jet black hair?"

"Yes. My sister met her today and claims she is trouble."

Finn laughed. "Any woman around you gets into trouble."

Bevon smiled. "That's true. Keep an eye on her, will ya? I don't want to be caught staring."

His brows rose, clearly not understanding the reason for the request. "Can do."

Finn retrieved his beer and slid it in front of Bevon just as another woman took the seat next to him—a woman whose perfume was overpowering. No thank you. He had his pick of women, and right now, Bevon really wanted to learn more about this fascinating witch-shifter newcomer.

Before he even finished his beer, the object of his interest slipped out the front door. That was quick. Had she identified him somehow? If so, it gave credence to his sister's concern. That meant it was time to do a little reconnaissance.

"Later." Bevon tossed down some Denlars and didn't bother waiting for his change.

"Don't tell me you're going to follow her?" Finn asked.

"At a distance." And only after cloaking himself.

Once outside, Bevon inhaled. The mystery woman was heading east. He teleported a few blocks down the main road and then surveyed the foot traffic, waiting for her to appear. It was possible she'd teleport to the hotel, but he hoped she wouldn't.

Ah, there she was. He liked how she constantly swiveled her head, clearly looking for danger. She held herself like a huntress, indicating she was trained—just like Tory and the rest of the dragon shifting Guardians.

Once she passed him, he stepped into a side alley and uncloaked himself. If she spotted him, perhaps they could strike up a conversation. If not, he'd gather as much intel about her as he could. Was he stalking her? In a way he was, but Bevon never would have considered it if his sister hadn't given him the warning.

Zulema entered the Edendale Hotel. Wanting to give her time to reach her room, Bevon waited a minute before going in after her. The clerk at the desk was wearing headphones, seemingly oblivious to the customers. If this man worked for his family, he'd be fired, but in this case, Bevon believed he could use it to his advantage.

The clerk looked up. "Can I help you?"

"I hope so. Some chick told me to meet her here. Her name is Zulema. About this tall with long, black hair. She's quite exotic looking."

"Yes, you must mean Zulema Garcia. She just went up to her room. I can give her a call if you wish."

Now wasn't the time to confront her. "On second thought, I'm sure I'll run into her tomorrow at the bar. Thanks anyway."

Bevon strolled out of there, happy that he'd learned her last name. Tomorrow, he'd ask one of Tory's cousins for help. Logan Caspian was a genius when it came to research. While Zulema Garcia might be a common name, he bet Logan could find her, especially if he could get a hold of her photo.

While Bevon didn't think this woman was any kind of real threat, he was curious what her story was. Was she out to harm him, or had his sister's sixth sense gone haywire? He certainly would have remembered if he'd met her before, so it wasn't a case of a scorned lover.

It didn't matter. It would be fun to find out who she really was.

Chapter Four

FOR THE NEXT few hours, Zulema tried to come up with a foolproof plan that would give her easy access once in Feyrion, but seeing Bevon Forrester tonight at the bar had unnerved her to the point where she couldn't think straight. And that was unacceptable.

To help center herself, she pulled out an old photo of her family to remind her of why she was doing this. Killing was never easy, even when her life was on the line, but to kill in cold blood was wrong. Given her circumstances though, she had to put her principles aside if she wanted to keep her mom and Maylora safe.

Zulema might not have been an expert at reading people, but it was hard to believe that Bevon was a murderer. He smiled. A lot. And he laughed. If he'd been a creep, he would have tried to pick up the woman who'd sat next to him at the bar, but Bevon seemed more focused on the bartender. She didn't want to think what that meant.

On the other hand, Bevon could indeed be a sociopath, convincing others to trust him so he could kill them. If the dossier was to be believed, Bevon Forrester was a womanizer, which might imply sociopath, but what did she know? The fact he didn't show any interest in the attractive woman sitting next to him put a pinprick of doubt into the legitimacy of the information.

Before she drew any firm conclusions, she needed to make sure she'd missed nothing else in the dossier. Only then would she make a trip to Feyrion. To ensure she was being thorough, Zulema pulled out her tablet and created a backstory for how she and Tamarella had met and why Zulema was going to Feyrion in the first place. This had to include how she came into possession of the medallion that created the portal. The most plausible explanation was that Tamarella had contacted her—through Derrick Valoric—and asked Zulema to visit. She would feign ignorance that her best friend had died, saying she'd been out of town and had only just returned.

It wasn't as if there was any way to communicate between realms other than by visiting, right? Or could these Feys telepath—like mates could?

There was the issue of explaining why no one in Feyrion had ever heard of Zulema. That meant she'd have to pretend to be Anna DeLeon, Tamarella's best friend, who hailed from a small town on the outskirts of Avonbelle Province.

According to the report, on one of Tamarella's visits to Valoric, she'd met Anna, who was a history teacher, as well as an amateur jewelry maker. According to what Derrick noted, Tamarella had been fascinated by the woman's passion and dedication, and the two had become fast friends. Valoric had written that their connection wasn't surprising since Tamarella never worked, yet she'd yearned for a life of service.

One good note was that Anna had never been to Feyrion, which made assuming her identity all the easier. Zulema could only hope the information was accurate, and that Tamarella hadn't displayed any photos of her and Anna during one of her visits.

If a photo didn't exist, Zulema believed it was possible that Tamarella had mentioned her friendship to someone close to her— her handmaiden, Betina Liliana, perhaps? Valoric said that Tamarella rarely told anyone when she was visiting Tarradon since her parents forbade it, saying it was too dangerous, but it wouldn't surprise Zulema if Tamarella told the handmaiden what Tarradon was like and who she'd met. Not many were able to experience two different realms.

The dossier said it was rumored that Bevon had actually been to Earth as well. She'd never met or heard of anyone who'd visited all three realms. Were murderers usually explorers? At the moment, she was beginning to doubt a lot of things.

But one step at a time. Zulema was quite happy with her plan to impersonate Anna DeLeon. At first, she thought she'd have an issue with money since Feyrion did not use Denlars, but the ever-thorough Derrick Valoric had included some Feyrion money in the folder. Not that Zulema planned to stay there for more than a few hours, but it might be necessary to bribe someone to show her where the treniam was grown.

The last thing to consider was where to create the portal. The dossier said it needed to be outside in a large space where no one would be watching. The real Anna DeLeon would probably visit Tamarella around noon, rather than late at night, which meant Zulema had to be extra careful when traveling in the daytime. Even though Zulema could cloak herself, it took a lot of effort.

One thing that Derrick omitted was a description of Feyrion, implying he might never have visited his mate on her home world. That was okay. She didn't need anyone questioning her about what Mr. Valoric looked like.

While Zulema had no intention of returning to the eternal flame, she'd spotted land on the outskirts of the forest where she could open a portal without any prying eyes.

With that last piece of the puzzle solved, Zulema showered and readied for bed. Tomorrow would be a historic day for her.

"FAY CLAIMS THIS mystery woman is out to harm you?" Kenton asked.

Bevon wasn't sure why he was so fixated on her, but from the moment he laid eyes on Zulema, his body had betrayed him. "So she says."

Tory leaned forward. Bevon had stopped over at their condo, located not far from Wings, before heading home for the night. "What did the woman say to give Fay that idea?" Tory asked.

"Nothing. Fay sensed the woman was troubled." He explained about her reaction to the Forrester name.

Tory shook her head. "Being troubled doesn't mean she plans to harm anyone. Besides, why you? Why not my mate? He is about to rule over a realm. Not that I wish that on him." Tory reached out and rubbed his brother's arm.

"I wish I knew. There's something going on, though. Zulema was already there when I arrived at the bar. Nothing more. She didn't even try to make contact."

"Meaning she didn't know it was you," Kenton said.

"Possibly, but I'm telling you, I instantly felt my whole body come alive."

Kenton chuckled. "You're like that with all hot women."

Bevon appreciated women, but this sensation was different. "It wasn't the same. My heart raced, and then there was this pressure on my chest."

Kenton's brows raised. "Don't tell me the universe has stopped rotating long enough for you to find your mate?"

Bevon laughed. "Hardly. I enjoy people too much to settle down with just one woman."

Kenton shook his head. "I never thought I'd find my mate either, but the moment I spotted Tory's black with yellow scales flying overhead, I was a goner." He skimmed a knuckle down her cheek and smiled. "She was all I could think about. Hell, I gave her a piece of my soul to save her."

Bevon looked over at Tory and Kenton. The love in their eyes was unmistakable. "It's not like that with Zulema," Bevon said, even though he wasn't sure if he believed it.

"Fine, then forget this Zulema woman."

"I will. Thanks for the brotherly advice."

After they chatted about everything but the raven-haired beauty, Bevon teleported back to the cabin in the woods—the cabin that was invisible to all but fellow Feys. After downing a few beers, he was no more able to forget Zulema than he could stop breathing. He doubted she'd managed to put a curse on him since they were in the same establishment for less than five minutes. Even he didn't know he'd be at Wings until the last minute.

Zulema couldn't have followed him there since he'd arrived after she did. He also teleported to Wings from the woods, which would have left no trace of his presence. He told himself that it was his sister's eerie warning that had him on edge, but he wasn't completely convinced. The only way to solve this problem was to follow Zulema tomorrow. If she was up to something, it wouldn't be hard to find out what.

THE NEXT MORNING, Bevon rose early, determined to get to the bottom of this Zulema issue. He teleported to Edendale and landed behind the hotel. When he was certain no one was about, he uncloaked himself. Even as he did, he worried that the good citizens of Avonbelle Province would freak seeing someone appear out of nowhere. Only Feys—and apparently some witches—could teleport. The ordinary citizen could not.

As much as Bevon wanted to go inside the hotel and wait for Zulema to come down through the lobby, he had the sense she'd remember him from the bar last night assuming she spotted him. She might even ask why he seemed to be following her. For that, he'd have no answer—other than to say his sister was worried about her.

"Are you following me?" said the silkiest voice he'd ever heard.

What? How had she snuck up on him without his knowledge? Something must have short-circuited his abilities. Bevon felt it in his bones who had said those words even before he turned around. He faced her and smiled. "Excuse me?"

"The front desk clerk told me that a man matching your description came in last night asking about me. Was that you?"

He wasn't good at lying. "Yes."

Zulema pulled back her shoulders, and he almost laughed. She looked like she was ready to go head-to-head in a battle with him. "Why did you want to speak with me?" she asked.

"I saw you at Wings last night." He held out his hand. "I'm Bevon Forrester. You met my sister, Fay, yesterday at the eternal flame."

"I did." Reluctantly, she shook his hand. She was cautious. Good.

He waited for her to continue, but she merely stared, almost daring him to tell her something important. "She's worried about you." That sounded lame.

"Fay doesn't even know me. We only spoke for a minute or two before she...disappeared."

Fay's changing from her human form to that of a Fairy would be disconcerting the first time anyone saw her do it. "She told me that your mother is sick."

Zulema's beautiful eyes hardened. That seemed to be a taboo subject. "She is, but it is none of her concern—nor yours for that matter."

Ouch. Pain radiated off this woman—a woman he wanted to get to know better. Normally, it would be to seduce her, but this time he wanted to know why she was holding in her emotions so fiercely, and why she was so full of despair. "Can I buy you a cup of coffee?" he asked.

"No, but thank you. I have an appointment."

Bevon never pushed. "Be safe."

Her smile was brief and appeared forced. Zulema spun around and took off. He knew women. If he attempted to follow her in the usual manner, she'd not be pleased.

Once Zulema was out of view, he cloaked himself and followed, hoping she couldn't sense his presence like he could hers.

She walked down the back alley for a block and then cut through to the main street. Bevon did the same, only when he stepped onto the sidewalk, she was nowhere to be seen. Either she'd teleported somewhere, or she'd entered a shop.

Bevon didn't want to be one of those stalker creeps, but he wanted to make sure she wasn't in any danger—from whom, he couldn't guess. So what if Zulema seemed to be able to take care of herself? He needed to see her to be certain.

He teleported around town, hoping to get a glimpse of the mystery woman, but she'd disappeared. That meant it was time for him to return to the forest and watch over the portal to Feyrion—after he had a little talk with Logan Caspian. The more information Bevon had on this mystery woman, the better.

Chapter Five

S EEING BEVON AGAIN troubled Zulema more than she wanted to admit. She had teleported from her hotel room to the back alley with the intention of grabbing a coffee before heading to the forest, but after seeing him, she'd changed her mind. Zulema needed to get as far away from Bevon Forrester as quickly as possible—or chance losing her nerve to kill him.

She would take his life if need be, but only after she was convinced he was the one who had murdered his cousin.

Perhaps she was naive, but did killers invite a woman out for coffee? It didn't matter. Most likely her indecision stemmed from the fact she didn't want to kill anyone. Even if Bevon Forrester was evil and mean, she might have a hard time shooting an arrow through his heart.

With her medallion firmly in her grasp, she teleported to the edge of the forest. Because there were fields along the edge, she was still a bit exposed. She had thought this would be a good choice, but dragons could fly overhead and spot her. Even if they did though, what could they do?

Nothing.

Decision made. This would be where she would create her first portal. Holding the medallion in the palm of her hand, she swung her arm three times to the right and then twice to the left. She honestly didn't have a lot of faith this would work, but when massive swirls of air appeared in front of her, Zulema's heart nearly gave out. She'd done it!

Not wanting the portal to disappear before she had the chance to enter, she stepped through it. This being her first portal trip, she had no idea what to expect.

She had to say it was rather uneventful. One second she was on the edge of a forest in Tarradon, and the next she was standing on top of a mountain range overlooking a lake. That being said, the view was unlike anything she'd ever seen. Not only were all of the trees thick and rich with color, the lake below was of the deepest blue. Every color in fact appeared to be super saturated, almost as if she was wearing a pair of glasses that intensified everything.

And the air? It seemed cleaner and sweeter than anything she'd ever smelled. Not only that, the temperature was perfect.

However, she hadn't come to sightsee. If she had, she would have planned to stay for weeks to get her fill of this beautiful land. There had been no mention of the species of animals she'd see, but she didn't want to chance upon some beast who was more powerful than a dragon.

Only then did it occur to her that her powers might not even exist in this realm. To test her worst nightmare, she attempted to shift. Success!

Since she needed to scope out some fields for this poisonous treniam plant, Zulema soared above the glimmering lake, and while tempted to dive into the clear waters, she wasn't sure how long she could remain in Feyrion before she was identified as an interloper. The last thing she needed was to be taken to their police station and questioned. On purpose, she hadn't taken any identification with her. Carrying a bank card or a driver's license with her real name on it would incriminate her, and she couldn't afford that. Too bad Derrick Valoric hadn't created some fake papers for her in the name of Anna DeLeon. Clearly, the man was not infallible.

Since he hadn't thought of everything, it meant she couldn't spend a lot of time searching for the plant—at least not until she understood what she was up against. While she flew over the realm, her breath was taken away many times from the sight of the rich farmland and the acres of abundantly colorful flowers. Zulema spent about an hour looking around, only to realize she was going to need help in locating this poisonous plant. For now, she'd table her search.

It was time to look for Tamarella's home and start investigating who might have killed her. This part of the dossier was a bit sketchy since it didn't indicate where to find the deceased woman's house— or castle. Surely, the townsfolk should be able to direct her to the Warnom's estate. If Tamarella was a princess, her home would be well-known.

Zulema shot upward for a better vantage point, hoping to spot a city where she could ask for directions. After flying for about fifteen minutes, she reached a large town. It wasn't the size of Edendale, but it would do. During her flight, she never spotted another dragon, which gave her some cause for concern. In case they didn't exist here, she landed in a field, shifted, and then teleported the rest of the way.

From all the stress created by this assignment, she could use a good cup of coffee and a friendly face. As long as she remembered her name was Anna DeLeon, she should be okay. This might not be her first undercover assignment, but it could turn out to be the most important.

To her surprise, the inside of the coffee shop looked remarkably like the one she had back home. Zulema walked up to the counter and ordered a black coffee. Some of the names were rather strange, so she stuck with a safe order. When her stomach grumbled, she pointed to a pastry. Paying went smoothly since she handed the woman the largest bill she had.

"Can I ask you something?" Zulema said to the girl cashing her out.

"Sure."

"I'm from Tarradon, and I just arrived. I was invited to the Warnom estate, only when I came through the portal, there was no one there to give me directions."

Her eyes widened. "I've never used a portal, but the Warnom's live east of here about fifteen minutes by car. You can't miss it."

"Thanks."

With her coffee and pastry in hand, Zulema took a seat near the window. She was curious to see what similarities there were between the realms as well as the differences. While she'd never heard that Feys were violent, she wanted to see for herself. Someone had killed the poor woman, though it was possible a non-Fey had been responsible.

People appeared out of nowhere on the sidewalk and then disappeared again. Teleporting seemed to be commonplace. Good. That would make moving about easier. Zulema was relieved when she spotted a few dragons overhead. That meant she wouldn't be considered a freak of nature.

She wasn't here to study the culture, though. Zulema needed to find the treniam and then determine if Bevon Forrester had killed his cousin.

After eating, Zulema walked to the edge of town to find a place to shift and take off. Hopefully, there weren't too many castles east of there, as it would be a bit embarrassing if she knocked on the wrong door. If that happened, at least, she had a good cover story.

She soared upward and then leveled off. Fifteen minutes by car was maybe ten minutes by air. When she spotted a castle, she landed in the field and then shifted. Zulema wished the dossier had mentioned if Anna DeLeon was a dragon shifter. Darn. That could be the one thing that might give away her false identity.

She was a short distance from the front of the castle when two guards teleported before her. "State your reason for being here," one of them said in a very commanding voice.

Zulema inhaled. She was ready. "I received a note from Princess Tamarella. She asked that I visit. I live on Tarradon." That came out stilted, but they had taken her by surprise.

At the mention of the other realm, the tension in their faces disappeared. "Do you have this note?" one of the guards asked.

"No. It was delivered by a friend of hers—a Derrick Valoric."

They stiffened. He didn't seem to be welcome here in Feyrion. "Come with me."

She followed. Having grown up rather poor, Zulema couldn't help but stare at the opulence. The castle was made of stone, but the many large windows seemed to be from a different era, not that the two realms should have the same design elements.

"Wait here," the guard said after they escorted her into the foyer.

Fresh flowers sat on the entry table and large paintings adorned the walls. A moment later, footsteps sounded down the marble hallway. A regal woman wearing a long, white gown, effortlessly moved toward her.

"I'm Tamarella's mother. Can I help you?"

"Nice to finally meet you. I'm Anna DeLeon, a friend of your daughter's in Tarradon. She asked that I visit. It sounded important. Is she here?"

The woman's lips thinned. "I'm sorry you came all this way. I'm afraid Tamarella died over a week ago."

Zulema planted a palm on her chest and sucked in a breath to show her surprise. "That's terrible. How did it happen?" It might give her some insight into how Bevon—or whoever had killed her—accomplished it. Valoric implied it had something to do with treniam.

"It appeared as if Tamarella rubbed treniam on her body and then slit her wrists—or so we were told." Tension riddled the woman's features.

Good. Her intel had been accurate. "But you don't think it was suicide, do you?"

"Absolutely not. My daughter would never disgrace the family like that. While she wasn't thrilled to mate with Tristan, she understood it was her duty." Her mother lifted her chin.

"I totally agree. I'm guessing you have a suspect for this murder?" Zulema held her breath, partially hoping she didn't say it was Bevon. Though if he were guilty, it would make her life easier since she knew where to find him.

"Not yet. Where are my manners? Please come into the drawing room. Would you care for a glass of camtandor?"

She had no idea what that was, but if it was offered, it would be rude to turn it down. "Yes, thank you."

She followed Tamarella's mother into the parlor. Convincing her that Zulema had known her daughter might prove to be her biggest test yet, so she had to be careful what she said. While Zulema wanted to ask a million questions about the daughter's death, she didn't want to raise suspicion. However, a good friend wouldn't sit idly by, now would she?

"I am still in shock," Zulema said. "Tamarella told me that Feys were kind of immortal."

"That's true. The treniam plant will weaken a Fey, but my daughter was only half Fey. I'm sure she told you that I'm a Fairy. We do not react the same way to treniam."

That piece of information had been left out of the file. It was all the more reason to suspect foul play. "I can't imagine the grief you must be going through. And Tristan? He must be beside himself."

At the mention of Tamarella's betrothed, her mother stiffened—just like the guards had when Zulema mentioned Valoric. "Tristan is devastated, for sure. The union would have united two powerful families."

How sad that love wasn't mentioned or even implied. "That is a shame." As much as she wanted to bring up Derrick Valoric's name, this probably wasn't the time.

"Tamarella spoke of a handmaiden, Betina. Did she see anyone go into Tamarella's room—assuming Tamarella died in the house?"

"My daughter died in her room, but Betina saw no one. She heard some kind of commotion, and when she went to check on my daughter, she found Tamarella on the floor, bleeding to death. Betina called us, but by the time my husband and I arrived, it was too late."

Zulema sighed. This time, it was a real reaction to the tragedy. "Could someone have snuck into the room, killed her, and left?" The castle seemed rather secure, but she bet a cousin could enter without notice.

The mother stared at Zulema for a moment. "Sneaking is not necessary when any Fey or Fairy can teleport to her room."

Many warlocks and witches could too, but she didn't mention that. "Of course."

A servant entered carrying a tray with two wonderful smelling drinks. She set it down and handed each of them a cup. Zulema sipped the hot brew and smiled. "This is delicious."

"Thank you."

"Are the authorities investigating Tamarella's death?"

"Not anymore. They ruled it a suicide—rather quickly, I'm afraid. However, I've asked Tristan to discretely ask around to see if he can find out her frame of mind at the time of her death and whether my daughter might have taken her own life. Tamarella wasn't always forthcoming with me." The mother's lips pinched. "And apparently not with Tristan either."

"You don't think he had anything to do with her death, do you?"

"Tristan? Absolutely not. He had everything to gain by them being together."

Was it possible Tristan wanted out of the union as much as Tamarella did? If Valoric was to be believed, Tamarella was in love with Valoric. Possibly, Tristan was in love with someone else too.

Zulema finished off her drink and stood. "Once more, I am so sorry this happened. I'll be on my way. Thank you for talking to me in your time of need."

"You're welcome to stay the night. We have room." Her smile came out weak.

Zulema tried to decide if her offer was sincere. If Zulema stayed, it might give her the chance to speak with Betina, and maybe even Tristan—assuming she could find out where he lived.

"That is very kind of you."

"Wonderful. Without Tamarella, this house has been empty. Where is your luggage?"

Shit. "I honestly wasn't planning on staying. If Tamarella needed me, I would have opened the portal once more and returned to

Tarradon to pick up a few things."

"Don't bother. I'll have Betina lend you a few of Tamarella's things. You two are about the same size."

Zulema didn't want to wear a dead woman's clothes, but to say no might look suspicious. "I'd appreciate that."

The mother rang a bell, and a servant appeared a minute later. "Yes, ma'am?"

"Can you find Betina and ask her to come here?"

"Of course."

Despite the unexpected turn of events, Zulema had to say this day couldn't have gone better. Good thing she hadn't found the treniam. Hiding it on her person might have caused her to be arrested—or worse, killed—assuming the person got the drop on her. Her ability to teleport, when no other dragon shifter she knew could, offered a wonderful ability to escape.

Chapter Six

"HERE'S A GOWN that Tamarella often wore at night," Betina Liliana said, holding up a beautiful shirt made from the softest material. "Don't worry. It's clean."

"Thank you." Because wearing the clothes of the recently deceased was a bit creepy, Zulema might just sleep in her underwear.

"Will there be anything else, Miss?"

"Just a question, that's all."

"Yes?"

"Her mother said you found Tamarella?"

Betina inhaled. "Yes. It was terrible. I was in total shock. I know everyone is saying it was suicide, but I know it wasn't." She looked around, acting as if she suspected someone would burst into the room at any moment.

"Why would you say that?"

"I heard a commotion in her room right before she died."

That matched up with what Tamarella's mother had said. "Which means someone was in her room and killed her, right?"

"That's what I think."

"Did you see who?"

"No. I rushed into her room, but no one other than Tam was there. All I saw was blood. So much blood." She sucked in a shudder. "Tamarella was barely conscious. I tried to stop the bleeding, but I couldn't. Her mouth opened and closed, as if she was trying to tell me something. When I leaned over, all she said was Bevon." Betina looked up. "He must have killed her."

Zulema's heart squeezed. "You believe her cousin killed her?"

"Perhaps."

This was how rumors got started. "Why? Had they been fighting? I mean, I've never met the man, but he lives on Tarradon, does he not?"

Betina nodded. "He does." She lowered her gaze. "I've only met him a few times myself, and he seemed nice. Because Tamarella rarely spoke of him, something must have happened."

That made no sense. "But why call out Bevon's name? Could she have wanted you to contact him for some reason?"

"Maybe, but why not called out Derrick's name or even Tristan's name for that matter?"

"Why indeed?" Zulema said.

"I know that Bevon and his brother, Kenton, showed up the next morning, but Bevon only stayed a few hours—just enough to provide comfort to the family."

That would imply he might not have been on Feyrion when Tamarella died, though coming and going seemed to be easy for a Fey. "If I'd murdered a woman, I might not be so anxious to stay long," I said.

"That's true."

Betina seemed to have thought this through. "You're sure she didn't kill herself?"

"I'm positive! She might have been in love with Derrick, but she knew her role in the family."

"I've never met Tristan. He was kind to her, right?" Even if Zulema had been Anna, Tamarella might not have been totally forthcoming to her.

Betina averted her gaze. "He was, but he too agreed to the arrangement under duress."

That was interesting. "Was there someone else in his life?"

"I don't know, ma'am. I'm just a servant." Her tone suddenly turned distant. She was hiding something.

"Thank you for speaking with me. I agree that Tamarella never would have killed herself. It wasn't in her. Besides, I don't think she would be the type to find a field of treniam, cut some, and carry it home."

"That was what I was thinking. Someone else had to have brought it here."

Her mind raced. "If that someone was a Fey, wouldn't it have harmed him, or her, too?"

"Yes, but perhaps this person wore gloves."

The girl had an answer for everything. "Again, thank you."

Betina nodded and left. Zulema didn't think she was any closer to learning whether Bevon was the killer than before she'd arrived.

"BEVON, WAKE UP!"

That was his sister's voice in his head. He roused. *"Tally?"*

His shy sister rarely contacted him. She'd made it clear that her life was on Feyrion and not on Tarradon, claiming Fay and Meena were capable of handling everything there, and that they didn't need her.

"Yes. I have something important to tell you."

He sat up and dragged a hand down his unshaven face. *"What is it, sweet sister?"*

"Fay told me about some raven-haired woman looking to harm you."

That again. *"She's harmless. I haven't given her a second thought."* No use causing his already nervous sister any more stress.

"Then why is she on Feyrion asking questions?"

Bevon flew out of bed, his heart beat accelerating. *"You must have the wrong woman. Zulema isn't Fey, and I certainly didn't let her through the portal."*

"Come see for yourself."

"Have you seen her?"

"No, but one of the Warnom staff mentioned it to one of our staff members that a visitor from Tarradon was here. She's claiming to be a friend of Tamarella's. Mother had sensed an intruder and found her at

Aunt Drina's house."

"Thank you for letting me know."

"Should I tell Mother you'll be visiting?"

Decisions, decisions. "I might."

With that, he steeled his mind against any further intrusion, at least until he had some coffee. With a swipe of a hand, he dressed and padded out to the kitchen. What was with this woman, Zulema Garcia, haunting him?

For once and for all, he needed to find out what she was up to. As he fixed breakfast, he tried to decide his best plan of attack. She might think he was of Fairy descent since his sister was one, but his larger size would hopefully clue her into his Fey heritage. He had no idea how much she knew about his culture. The fact she'd found her way to Feyrion—a realm most people weren't even aware existed—implied this was no ordinary adversary. But did that knowledge give him an advantage of any kind?

Perhaps he'd been naïve in thinking this woman was merely sad and misguided. Bevon needed to proceed with caution. Even though he'd gone to Feyrion for a very short visit after the death of his cousin a week ago, he would return, visit for a bit, and then check in on his aunt, who was still reeling after Tamarella's tragic death.

If he thought by staying after his cousin's death that he could have helped, he would have, but everyone seemed to think his cousin had committed suicide. While he hadn't been around Tamarella much in the last couple of years, she'd never felt sorry for herself. How had she changed that much? Surely, someone in his family would have mentioned her altered personality.

"Kenton? A moment of your time?" Bevon telepathed.

A second later, his brother was by his side. "You sound worried. I thought a face-to-face might be in order."

"Not worried. Concerned."

"They mean the same thing."

"Fine. I am a bit disturbed. Happy?" He explained he received a message from Tally.

Kenton grabbed a coffee cup out of the kitchen cabinet and poured himself a drink. The fact he didn't swipe his hand and create the drink implied he was becoming more accustomed to life here.

"Are you sure that this woman who arrived at our aunt's home is your Zulema?"

Zulema didn't belong to him. "Yes. Or at least I'm pretty sure she is."

"Good. Now that we've had time to think about Tamarella's death, do you believe she took her life because she was being forced into a marriage with Tristan?" Kenton asked.

Bevon had met Tristan. The man wasn't someone he would necessarily go out of his way to hang out with, but he seemed a nice enough sort of soul—for a warlock. "Not really, mostly because Tamarella wasn't highly rebellious. She wanted what was best for both families."

"I agree."

Bevon downed the rest of his coffee. "I guess it's time I take a little visit home. I trust you can man the portals?"

"Of course. Besides, we don't need you distracted by a woman for a reason other than enjoyment."

Bevon laughed. "So true, brother. So true."

Once Kenton left, Bevon created a portal to his home world. As much as he enjoyed Tarradon and all that it had to offer, he was the first to admit that Feyrion was quite glorious. The weather was always perfect, the air pure, and the colors stimulating. Yes, there were pockets of evil, but his portion of Feyrion was quite special.

He teleported straight to his parents' home. Out of habit, he knocked and then teleported into the living room. *"Tally?"* he telepathed.

His sister appeared next to him. "You came!" She hugged him, which was not her usual greeting.

"Why wouldn't I? Did something else happen you failed to mention?"

"No, and I want to keep it that way."

Like all Fairies, they seemed incapable of getting to the point. "Tell me what you know."

"Not much other than some dragon shifter swooped in and ended up being invited to stay the night at Aunt Drina's house. Here's the thing. She said her name was Anna DeLeon."

Bevon laughed. "You mean I came here because of the wrong woman?"

"No, that is what has me worried. She is claiming to be a friend of Tamarella's."

"Maybe she is. Why do you think she's Zulema?"

"She has long black hair and is rather exotic looking."

He shook his head. "Your imagination is getting the best of you. We know that our cousin visited Tarradon because she fell in love with that no good Derrick Valoric. She probably met many people."

Tally glanced away. "I know."

"I'm sure more than one pretty woman in the world has long, black hair."

"Perhaps."

He felt bad that Tally was distressed. "I'll tell you what. I'll visit Aunt Drina to offer my sympathies once more. I'll mention that I heard that Tamarella's friend from Tarradon was there visiting. I'll see her for myself. Okay?"

A small smile lifted her lips. "Thank you, but be careful."

"Of what? She can't hurt me."

"I know, but you have a fragile heart."

He laughed. "Me? I've never fallen for a woman."

"Not yet, my dear brother. Not yet."

"What does that mean?"

Before she could answer, their mother arrived. "Bevon! This is such a nice surprise."

"Mother."

"Tally told me both she and Fay are worried about you."

He needed to solve this once and for all. "I'm sure it's a case of mistaken identity."

"I hope so, but I'm glad I am able to see you again—and so soon. I hope that brother of yours hasn't gotten into trouble."

"Kenton? Hardly. Tory keeps him in line," Bevon said. Both understood that Kenton would do nothing to besmirch the Forrester's good name.

"Happy to hear that. I know you want to resolve this issue, so be on your way. My sister is understandably beside herself since she's taking the blame for Tamarella's death, you know."

"How so?"

His mother furrowed her brows. "If she had allowed Tamarella to follow her heart—misguided as many think it was—my niece might not have killed herself."

"Are you convinced it was suicide?"

"Honestly? I'm not sure. On the one hand, it's easier to believe that Tamarella was responsible for her own death. If someone killed her, that someone should pay."

"If she was murdered, who do you suspect?"

She shook her head. "No one. Tristan, while not madly in love with her, understood his role. With Tamarella dead, the Warnoms and the Stantons will never be as powerful as they could have been."

Bevon did love a good mystery. It added spice to life. "Could someone else have wanted to marry Tristan and decided she needed Tamarella out of the way?"

"You'd have to ask Tristan."

"No one is investigating this?"

"Not any more. One of our most powerful witches examined Tamarella. She said that Tam was weak from treniam and then died from blood loss from her slit wrists."

That proved nothing. His cousin was part Fairy and shouldn't be as susceptible to the deadly plant. He huffed out a breath. "If Tam spread the treniam on her body, don't you think she'd be too weak to harm herself?"

His mom's mouth opened. "I don't know. That is an excellent point. It's possible that she slit her wrists and then wanted to quicken her death by rubbing her arms with that plant."

"Did anyone find the plant next to her?" Even if she'd disposed of it in the trash, someone would have seen it.

"We should ask my sister. Would you like me to come with you when you speak to her?"

He almost laughed, but the situation was anything but funny. "I'm quite capable of doing this. I'll be back shortly."

After he hugged his mother goodbye, Bevon teleported over to his aunt and uncle's estate. He knocked, because teleporting into their home might be too disruptive. It didn't matter that when he and Kenton were kids, they used to do it all the time.

One of the staff answered. "Master Bevon. Come in."

He entered, not sure how to approach the delicate subject of their house guest. The safest tactic would be to speak with his aunt. "Is Aunt Drina here?"

"Yes, sir."

He could have telepathed to her, but this approach seemed better.

A few seconds later, his aunt appeared. "Bevon! This is such a nice surprise. Come into the living room. Can I get you something to drink?"

"No, thank you." He followed her inside and sat on the sofa next to her. "I wanted to see how you were holding up."

She clasped his hands. "Doing the best I can, but you didn't have to come all this way to check up on me."

"I know, but I wanted to. Mother said the case is closed?"

"Yes. They're ruling it a suicide."

Was that because it was easier or because it was the truth? "What do you think?"

She shook her head. "I don't know. I can't believe Tamarella would kill herself. She called your name right before she died. Do you know why?"

His pulse shot up. "My name? No. I hadn't even spoken with Tamarella for months."

"That's odd."

"It is. I know that Tam had treniam in her system. Did anyone find the plant discarded anywhere?"

His aunt looked confused. "No, and they should have. I'll ask the staff."

The killer probably took it with him. "Before you do, Tally told me a friend of Tamarella's is here. Maybe she knows more," he said.

"I don't think so. Anna didn't even know that Tamarella had died."

Bevon was very curious how this Anna made it into the realm without passing through his portal, but that was a question he needed to ask her. "Would it be okay for me to speak with Anna? I might be able to piece some things together. She might know why Tam called out my name."

"Of course. She's in the backyard, I believe."

Bevon wasn't sure it was particularly wise to let a stranger have the run of the house, but it was not his place to say. "Thank you. I'll check." He stood, leaned over, and kissed his aunt's cheek.

Bevon teleported to the back of the house where he spotted a woman near the edge of the property who seemed fascinated with the flowers. His pulse raced. It was her!

It wasn't until he was within ten feet of her that she spun around, and the look on her face was one of recognition. Gotcha! Let's see how she explains this deception.

Chapter Seven

ZULEMA HAD BEEN so engrossed in the beauty of the flowers that she hadn't sensed another person's presence until a moment ago when her senses shot to high alert. She spun around. It didn't matter if she'd been trained to show no surprise, her body betrayed her big time. Her face flushed, and she was sure her eyes flashed purple.

It was Bevon Forrester. For one second, she wished she could create her crossbow out of thin air, but then she realized after speaking with Tamarella's mother, as well as her handmaiden, something was off. Even the dying girl's last word didn't necessarily implicate Bevon as her killer. It was possible, she wanted to warn him—of what Zulema had no idea. Or was she wishing Bevon was innocent so she wouldn't have to kill him—assuming she could?

Decision time. Should she pretend as if she'd never seen him before or be honest? From the lack of surprise on his face, he knew exactly who she was.

Being honest—at least about her identity—might be for the best. "Bevon, I didn't expect to see you here."

One brow rose. "Me? I'm a Fey, and my parents rule here. I think it is you who owes me an explanation as to why you are here." For once, his cute cockiness wasn't present.

Think!

"A while back, Tamarella asked me to visit her. I was out of town and only just received the message. You can imagine how shocked I was to find she'd died."

"Is that so?" He chuckled.

Nothing was funny about what she'd said. "Yes."

"Tell me this. What color hair did my cousin have?"

Oh, shit. That was one piece of information Derrick Valoric had forgotten to include, which she found particularly odd. He should have included a photo of the woman he was supposed to have loved.

Zulema had three choices. Since his cousin's mother had blonde hair, as did Bevon, she went with that. "Blonde."

He shook his head. "Sorry, honey. You lose." He stepped closer. "Tell me why you're really here. Fay claims you're out to harm me." He held up a hand. "Not that you could, but I am curious why you think you are capable of taking a Fey's life?"

Zulema had one goal: to keep her mother and sister safe. To do that, she feared she'd have to kill an innocent man, but even if she had a handful of treniam, she didn't believe she had it in her to use it.

"Fine. I'm here on a mission."

He crossed his arms and smiled. "Is that so? Describe this mission."

There was a bench off to the side. "Mind if we sit?" she asked. "This could take a while."

"By all means, just as long as you can prove you don't have a stash of treniam on you."

She patted both of her two pockets to show they were empty. "I don't."

He motioned they sit. When Bevon sat next to her, her skin caught fire. Sure, the guy was super hot, but it shouldn't have been enough to unnerve her this much. Maybe it was the air here that was throwing off her senses.

"Tell me. And don't lie."

This was going to be very hard. "I am from Tarradon. My job there is that of a bodyguard."

He didn't flinch. "I had an acquaintance check you out. He learned that. Thank you for being honest."

Shit. Did he know about Derrick Valoric? If the Zon was mated to his cousin, he might. "Two days ago, I was kidnapped."

Bevon's cheer immediately evaporated. "Were you hurt?"

"Not really." She explained about her meeting with the virtual Valoric. "He told me that I have two weeks to kill you, or he'll kill my very sick mother and my only sister."

He nearly choked. "Why me?"

"Your cousin's mate is convinced you murdered her."

His mouth opened. "I wasn't even on the realm at the time of her death."

"That wasn't what I'd heard."

He leaned back. "Tell me what you know."

She explained how Betina, the handmaiden, heard Tamarella yell. "There seemed to have been some kind of commotion. When she arrived, no one was there, but Tamarella was bleeding to death."

"I agree that I could have teleported to her room, but if I'd touched the treniam, I, too, would have become deathly ill."

"I thought of that, but you could have worn gloves."

"I'll give you that," he said. "Was this treniam found next to the body?"

"Not that I know of."

"If no one found any, then I might think the killer was not a Fey. It also implies my cousin didn't commit suicide."

Zulema liked his logic, but it wasn't without its flaws. "This non-Fey would have to have been rather savvy to even find this poisonous plant. It doesn't seem to grow wild around here."

"For good reason," he said. "You won't find any in this area."

Maybe it was good that she hadn't been counting on locating it without help. "My father was a warlock—a powerful one—and as such, I inherited his ability to teleport. From what I've seen, very few non-Fey can."

"That's true, which narrows down our field. That being said, I know of four women in Avonbelle who can teleport—ah, make that five women. They aren't Feys, Fairies, or your standard witch. However, they only do good."

Intriguing. "What do you plan to do now?" she asked.

"I, for one, do not like that someone is trying to frame me for something I clearly didn't do. However, I understand your dilemma. If I don't die, your mother and sister will."

"Exactly."

He leaned closer, and it was almost as if he was able to hypnotize her with his eyes. "What do you say we work together?"

She blurted out a laugh. "Work together? Doing what?"

"If Derrick wants to know who killed Tamarella, we need to find this killer. It should be quite obvious that I can ask as many questions as I'd like and not raise suspicion. You were here for a few hours, and my sister contacted me to say our family had a new visitor. In other words, you aren't invisible. And that should scare you."

"What do you mean?"

"I did not kill Tamarella, and I'm pretty sure she didn't commit suicide. That means the killer is still out there. He or she doesn't need you snooping."

Her blood pressure spiked. "You do have a point."

"I know."

"Did Fay tell you that I was here?" Did she frequently travel between realms?

"No, it was Tally, another one of my sisters, but Fay clearly warned her of your dangerous intent."

His family was more connected than she'd first believed, but it didn't mean they knew everything. "We can't just point a finger at the guilty party. Derrick will demand to see a dead body."

"Fine. We'll figure out who killed my cousin and give him that person to do with as he chooses."

"Will this guilty party be alive or dead?"

"Alive."

Bevon was naïve. "This person would have to confess to the crime, or Derrick won't believe you."

"You're right. What do you propose?"

"I'm not sure. I do know that Derrick—or rather the Zon,

which is the organization he is associated with—says he will know if and when you are dead, so I can't just tell him I killed you."

"Did he mention if he wants me dead because he has a vendetta against me, or does he believe I really did kill my own cousin?"

"That I don't know. Have you interacted with Derrick before?"

"I've met him once, but things were cordial between us. It's possible he's upset that my family has money, and his might not."

That was a stretch. "What about the safety of my family? This Derrick person might not believe I am doing enough to kill you. He gave me two weeks, but who is to say he won't kill one of them to let me know that he means business."

He sat there for a minute, looking out over the vast estate. "I say, we nab your family and teleport them here, where they will be safe."

"That won't work," she said.

"Why not?"

"My mother is very ill. The trip could kill her."

He faced Zulema. "If we don't remove her from harm, Derrick might kill her anyway. Besides, teleporting only takes seconds. Did you feel anything when you went through the portal?"

It had only lasted a second or two. "No."

"See? I'll personally see to her safety."

She stared at him. He was too good to be true, which meant he wasn't. This had to be some kind of trap. "Why are you being so nice?"

Bevon laughed. "Really? I like life. A lot. I also don't want to have to look over my shoulder all the time. Killing me is hard, but hurting me isn't. I do bleed like everyone else."

She didn't know that. "Oh."

"I figure if your mother and sister are safe here, you will be able to focus on the task at hand. In fact, you'll be helping me stay out of trouble if we can find the real killer."

He sure had an odd way of turning things around. "I get it, but if we find the killer quickly, we might not have to move my family."

He shook his head. "I don't know much about Derrick, but I

don't trust him. Kidnapping you tells me he is not good. To be safe, let's free your mother and sister. You probably are unaware, but Feyrion is known for healing people when others can't. My mother is very powerful."

Her pulse soared. "Your mother is a healer?"

He grinned. "My mother is the queen of Feyrion with powers even I don't understand."

Her pulse soared. "Really?"

"Really."

She would be stupid to turn him down. "Okay."

"Okay, what?"

"Okay, let's save my family. If I know they are safe, I will be better prepared to help look for the killer." Having Bevon by her side would eliminate her need to sneak around. She hissed in a breath. "Should I still pretend to be Anna, Tamarella's friend?"

That cute gleam returned to his eyes. "You're admitting to that deception?"

"Yes, and I'm sorry, but it was the only way not to raise suspicion."

"You might be right. We will have to tell them, but later. Right now, we need to return to Tarradon."

She liked the sound of that. "Now?"

"No time like the present." Bevon looked to the side and then nodded slightly. "I just telepathed to my mother I would be leaving, but that I would be returning shortly with your mother who needs care."

This was too good to be true. "Thank you." She reached out and touched his hand, but immediately withdrew it. In that moment, it was as if he'd entered her soul. Zulema cleared her throat. "Do you think I could have killed you if I'd tried?"

One brow rose. "Planning to change your mind?"

"No. It is idle curiosity."

"To answer your question, it's not very likely. As you know, you'd have to find treniam, and that would be no easy chore. Now that you've told me you might reconsider, you wouldn't get the chance to. I would have you arrested and thrown in jail for the rest of your life. I am a prince after all."

Oh, shit. Valoric should have mentioned that fact. Her stomach did a somersault at the thought of incarceration. "You would throw me in jail?"

"Nah. You're too pretty to end up in jail." He slapped his thighs and stood. "Do you want to save your mother or what?"

She had to decide whether to trust him or not.

Yes, trust him, her dragon said, finally speaking up about the topic.

Are you sure?

Very.

"Yes." She couldn't help but smile.

If she believed his family to be all powerful, she didn't stand a chance at killing him anyway. Derrick Valoric had to know that, so why demand that she kill Bevon? Nothing was making sense.

"Good. Where is your mom?"

"In a nursing home on the far end of Avonbelle Province."

"Before we head out, I want you to meet my mom so you can rest easy that your mother will be in good hands."

Just as she was about to thank him, he reached out and touched her arm. A moment later, Zulema was in a grand living room. "You live here?" she whispered.

"Not any longer. Now, only my parents and my sister, Tally, do."

A regal looking woman, who was diminutive like Fay, entered the room. "You must be...?"

Bevon smiled. "This is Zulema Garcia, Mother. Yes, she was pretending to be Tamarella's friend Anna, but she had little choice. She was sent by Derrick Valoric to kill me."

"Kill you?"

"Yes, but that is in the past. Before we take care of that detail, we need to save her family. When we return, I will explain more fully."

Her mother turned to Zulema and smiled. "So nice to meet you. Zulema is such a pretty name."

Zulema's heart swelled. "Thank you, Queen Forrester." She hoped that was her royal title.

His mother chuckled. "Please call me, Arianna."

Really? "Okay."

"We need to go, Mother."

"I'll be waiting." She smiled and then hugged her son.

Zulema's heart swelled at the shared affection between them. There was a time when her mother was as gracious and loving. Maybe soon, she would be again.

Zulema wanted to thank his mom, but she didn't get the chance before she found herself outside. "A little warning next time?" she asked.

"If we could communicate telepathically, I'd oblige."

True. While Zulema had the medallion that Derrick had given her pinned to the inside of her shirt, she'd leave the portal crossing to the expert.

After a few arm circles, one appeared. "After you," he said with a devilish grin. If he sent her someplace unpleasant, she'd teleport out and then make a portal to Tarradon.

Where she landed was no jail. It was a house. Bevon stepped behind her. "Let me grab a beer, and we can discuss how to free your family."

"You live here?"

"I do."

Zulema couldn't believe how wrong she'd been about this man. Damn, Derrick Valoric.

Chapter Eight

BEVON NEVER BROUGHT a woman to his house, but Zulema was special. To what extent, he wasn't sure. He'd always been the kind to help others, but he seemed more connected to her than normal.

"She's your mate," his mother telepathed out of the blue. *"Treat her well."*

My mate? His pulse soared at the possible confirmation. He pulled a beer from the fridge not quite ready to respond to his mother—or willing to believe it might be true, despite his body and mind telling him it was. He almost chuckled thinking about a conversation that might take place years from now:

How did you and mom meet? his son would ask.

She was assigned to kill me.

For real? What did you do to piss her off? he'd ask.

Not her. I upset someone else who hired your mom.

Why didn't she succeed?

I charmed her.

"You're smiling," Zulema said. "Want to share? I could use some levity right about now."

He certainly wasn't going to tell her that mental thought. "It's nothing." He waved the beer. "Want one?"

"Sure."

He hadn't expected that answer, but he was delighted, nonetheless. Bevon handed her the one he had in his hand and pulled out another one.

"How do you know?" he asked his mother, now that he'd had a

moment to collect his thoughts.

"Mothers know. Don't keep her waiting." And then she was gone.

"You okay?" Zulema placed a hand on his arm.

Damn. "Yes. My mother just telepathed me, and I got a little distracted."

"Is everything all right?"

"Yes. She wanted to make sure we were okay." One brow rose. Zulema did not believe him, but she thankfully dropped the subject. He motioned they sit at the table. "Tell me about this facility where your mother is staying."

"Do you have a piece of paper and a pencil?"

He swiped a hand and voilá, it appeared. She looked up with genuine awe in her eyes. "I had no idea you were so powerful."

His ego ballooned. Many comebacks were on the tip of his tongue, but Zulema didn't seem like the type to appreciate them. "I don't really think about it." He nodded to the paper. "Give me as much detail about the layout of the hospital as you can."

"I'll try." To his delight, Zulema was quite the artist.

"Do you know your mother's schedule for when the doctors show up?"

"I thought Feys could remain invisible."

He laughed. "You have done your homework. Normally, I would teleport in, grab her, and teleport out, but if she is hooked up to any IV's, it might take longer. Besides, having someone invisible work on your mom might scare her into cardiac arrest."

Zulema almost smiled. "You're right. I'll need to come with you. Mom will need me to assure her we are moving her for her own good. And yes, she is attached to some IVs."

"What about your sister? It's not feasible to transport all of us to Feyrion at once, which is why you'll need to let her know we'll come back for her as soon as we can."

"I hate to prioritize like that, but I understand."

He liked her rational side. "Did Derrick mention if he had Maylora under surveillance?" It might alter his plans.

Her hands stilled. "No, but what if he does? I'm sure he knows where she lives. He seems to know everything."

Not everything. "I'd be guessing, but Derrick probably figures your mom would be the easier of the two to snatch. If we warn your sister, kidnapping her would make it more difficult for him."

"Then I'll do that."

"Good. Can she teleport?" he asked.

"No. Only my dad and I can—or rather he could. He's passed."

"I'm sorry."

"Me, too."

"As much as I want to save your mom and your sister now, we'll have a better chance under cover of darkness."

"And risk less chance of the nurses and doctors walking in on us."

"Yes. What do you say we grab something to eat and then leave around ten tonight? I imagine your mom will be left alone to rest for a few hours around that time."

"Sounds good. I'll have to tell the head nurse at least. I don't want her to worry."

That was smart. "Do you trust her?"

"Completely."

He checked his watch. "I imagine you'll want to clean up. How about I meet you in the hotel lobby in two hours? We'll eat and go."

She smiled and something inside him melted. His mother couldn't be right, could she? Was Zulema his mate? She wasn't drooling over him, and he always thought it went both ways.

"Sounds good."

She disappeared, and just like that, the lights seemed to dim, and his pulse slowed. Once they saved her mother and sister, they'd have a talk.

ZULEMA APPEARED IN her hotel room and immediately dropped

onto the bed. What the hell had just happened? Had she really agreed to work with the man she was supposed to murder? After meeting him, and seeing his extensive powers, her attempt would have been a suicide mission. Was that the plan all along? For her to die? Why though? It wasn't as if Derrick Valoric knew her, although he claimed to appreciate her talents. That, in and of itself, was a scary thought. She certainly didn't want him to demand she work for him on an ongoing basis.

Enough worrying about what might happen. She needed to concentrate on freeing her mom. First things first: take a shower. Zulema hoped it would give her a clearer head so she'd know how to proceed.

Under the hot steaming water, a plan materialized regarding her sister. She'd call Maylora and tell her the truth. Sure, she'd be upset, but appearing at her house with Bevon in tow would freak her out more. Zulema could almost picture the conversation.

Hey, Maylora. Remember I had to be out of town for a while? Her sister would nod. *My assignment was to assassinate a man—this man.* At that point, Maylora would either scream, faint, or try to run. None of those options would be helpful. Not wanting Derrick to spot her at her sister's, the moment Zulema finished showering, she called Maylora.

"You're back!" her sister said with such cheer that Zulema almost changed her mind about telling her that her life was about to change—at least for a bit.

Starting this conversation would be difficult. "I am, but something came up again that I need your help with."

"Of course."

"How is Mom, by the way?"

"Pretty much the same."

She hadn't expected there to be a big change in only two days. "Good. Listen, my job took me…to another part of the realm." It was a little lie.

"Okay."

"I met a man there who believes he can help Mom get better."

Maylora didn't say anything for a few seconds. "Really? Is he some kind of doctor?"

"No, he's a Fey." The closer she stuck to the truth, the better. "His mother has exceptional powers—as in healing powers."

"I see."

Her sister's hesitation implied she didn't believe her. "Tonight, Bevon and I are going to transport Mom to his home."

"You can't do that. She needs constant care."

"Yes, she does, but where she is right now isn't helping. Trust me, I have to do this. But there's more to the story. I don't have time to give you all of the details right now. What I need from you is to pack a small bag. Bevon and I will return and take you to be with her."

"I have a job, remember?"

"Yes. How about composing an electronic message to them so they don't worry when you don't arrive at work tomorrow, but don't tell them where you are going or anything."

"Zulema, you're scaring me."

She huffed out a breath. "Fine. Do you want to know the whole truth? It isn't pretty."

"Of course."

Her sister didn't really mean it, but Zulema needed her to understand. "A bad person demanded that I do something evil—as in kill someone. If I don't do it, they will kill you and Mom. It's why we need to take her someplace safe since I refuse to carry out the contract."

Silence.

"You're kidding, right?" Maylora asked.

"I wish I were."

"I thought you were a bodyguard. Are you saying, you are now an assassin for hire?"

Zulema blew out a breath. Perhaps she'd been wrong in keeping her sister in the dark for so long. "I am a bodyguard, but a few days ago, I was kidnapped by a group of warlocks who call themselves the Zon. I really don't know more than that, other than they aren't nice people."

"And they would kill me?"

"Possibly, so please pack and don't answer the door for anyone. Bevon and I will teleport to you when the time comes."

"How did you meet this Bevon guy?" her sister asked.

"I promise I will fill you in once we are all safe. Right now, I need to meet him to solidify our plan. We should be at your place a little after ten."

"Okay, but I don't like any of this. Did you warn Mom?"

Zulema inhaled deeply. "No. The less she knows, the better."

Maylora's inhale was loud. "I'll be ready."

"Thank you."

Zulema disconnected and breathed a sigh of relief. If she'd told her sister that Bevon had been the intended target, Maylora probably would have refused to go.

Not knowing how long she'd be in Feyrion, Zulema packed her things and asked the desk to keep her suitcase in the back room until her return. Because she assumed she'd be staying for some time on Feyrion, she tossed some toiletries and two changes of clothes in her backpack.

She'd just sat down in the lobby when Bevon strode in. He'd showered and changed. While she liked his hair down, he'd pulled it back and looked sexy as hell. As if he wanted to impress her, he'd put on a rather form-fitting navy-blue shirt. Oh, my. He'd succeeded in heating up her inner dragon.

Not wanting to let him know that he seemed to alter her physically whenever he was near, Zulema stood, slipped on her backpack, and slowly walked over to him. "Hi."

He grinned. "Hi, to you. Thank you for not skipping town."

That made her laugh. "Why would I do that? You're helping me."

He shrugged. "My sisters accuse me of being oblivious to reading between what a woman says and what she wants."

"I can't help you with other women, but I'm rather straightforward."

"Good to know. Ready?"

"Yes. I'll let you pick the dinner place since I'm new here."

"Do you prefer fish or steak?" he asked.

She rarely had the funds to afford eating out. "I like both."

"Then may I suggest the Highlanders Steakhouse?"

"Sounds good." Derrick Valoric would have a fit if he knew his money would be spent on paying for her to dine with Bevon Forrester.

Hopefully, if the Zon were watching her, they would think she was trying to get close to Bevon so that she could kill him. Little did they know that was not her plan at all.

Because teleporting wasn't common on Tarradon, they walked to the restaurant. The weather wasn't as balmy as it was on Feyrion, but she was okay with that. The cooler air would help to keep her senses sharp. The stroll would also give her time to make sure she wasn't making the biggest mistake of her life by trusting this man. Bevon Forrester was powerful. He'd demonstrated that many times over. If he and Derrick ever went head-to-head, Zulema had no doubt Bevon would be the victor.

Once they arrived at the restaurant, Bevon asked for a table in back, probably to make sure no one overheard any part of their plan to foil the Zon.

"Care for some wine?" he asked once they were seated.

As much as she could use a glass to help relax her for what they were about to do, Zulema had to watch her expenses. "I'm good."

"You sure? You look like you could use some. I'm buying if that's what is worrying you?"

Her mouth opened a bit. "I know that your sister is intuitive, but can you read minds?" Maybe that was how he seemed to see through her.

He laughed. "Oh, honey, if I could do that, I'd have so much fun with people. No. I can't. A cousin in my brother's mate's family is a genius at finding information on people. Only because Fay cautioned me about you did I ask Logan to check up on you."

Her mind spun. She didn't like where this was headed. "You researched me?"

"You researched me," he shot back.

"Technically Derrick did, but I get it. What did your friend find out?" Zulema had worked hard to keep a low profile.

"You're an expert markswoman, you basically see to it that your family is taken care of, and you don't seem to take any time for yourself—as in you don't have a personal life."

That was impossible for anyone to know. "You're making that up."

He grinned. "I might not be as intuitive as my Fairy sisters, but I know women. That last part was my personal observation."

Bevon implied she was some inexperienced virgin, and she was not. She just hadn't had time to date much. "I'm a bodyguard by profession. It doesn't lend itself to going to parties nor having a lot of time to go on vacation."

"That is a shame. I bet it doesn't pay all that well either."

Despite her training, heat rushed up her face. Zulema sat up straighter. "I do okay for myself, but my mother's care is not free."

He instantly sobered. "I'm sorry. That must be very hard on you. Does your sister work?"

She huffed out a laugh. "You don't know?"

"Ouch. I didn't ask Logan to do a deep family dive. I only wanted to know your capabilities."

"Don't tell me you were actually worried I could harm you?" He'd basically said he was indestructible.

"Not really, but as I said, I do bleed."

She smiled. "I'll keep that in mind."

Chapter Nine

DINNER WASN'T WHAT Zulema had expected. Up to now, Bevon hadn't been all that serious, but the moment they discussed how they were going to whisk her mother away from the nursing home, he'd sobered, acting as if this mission was the most important one in his life.

For Zulema, that meant a lot.

"Go over the plan once more," Bevon said. "We have to be on the same page."

She inhaled. "I'll do the teleporting since I know where I'm going. We'll land outside the nursing home and walk in."

He shook his head. "I think it would be better if we just appear in your mom's room."

"What if a nurse or doctor is there?"

"Hmm. That could pose a problem," he said.

"I'd rather follow protocol and sign in."

"You know best."

Her mind spun. "First, we'll talk to the head nurse to warn her that we'll be transferring my mother to a safer place. I'll even tell her that there has been a threat on her life. If a doctor or nurse is there, we'll wait until she is finished."

It looked like Bevon was holding in a smile. "I like your logistical mind. That works for me."

The logistics were still a bit unclear even to her—and she'd come up with them. "Can you create a portal inside the hospital room, or should we teleport her outside?" Zulema didn't know the extent of his talents.

"I can create a portal inside a room, but I suspect it might cause some damage. Let's go with your second method."

"Okay."

Their meal arrived and she dug in. "Mmm. This is incredible."

Zulema hadn't meant to moan, nor did she want him to think she'd never eaten an expensive meal before, but she didn't eat in these kinds of restaurants unless her client was paying.

"It is good, but didn't you sample some of the food on Feyrion while you were there?"

"I wasn't there for long. I think I ate some crackers. Your aunt served me some drink that kind of tasted like tea. It was delicious but very different from anything I've ever tasted before."

"That might have been camtandor. It is a delicacy."

"Yes! That was it."

"It comes from an exotic plant we grow on my homeland. It is something I miss here on Tarradon."

"Why don't you grow some here then? The forest is a fertile place."

His brows rose. "Grow, as in dig up the earth and plant something?"

From the sparkle in his eye, he was kidding her. "Is that beneath your station, Prince Forrester?"

He guffawed. "I don't think anyone has called me prince in years."

Now she was curious. "Why is that?"

He shrugged. "My brother is next in line to be king. I, for one, couldn't be happier. Having to meet with the powers-that-be to discuss strategies would bore me to death. Since I don't return home very often, there is no one to call me prince. It's not something I mention when in Edendale."

That made sense. "If gardening isn't in your wheelhouse, what do you like to do?" Zulema had no idea why the man intrigued her, but he was different from anyone she'd ever met.

"Enjoy life. I like people and pleasure."

"That sounds…empty," she said.

"Ouch, princess."

Princess? Well, she was one for speaking her mind. "Convince me I'm wrong."

He leaned back in his chair, picked up his glass of wine, and tossed some back. "Challenge accepted. I like to help people." He nodded to her. "Case in point."

"That doesn't count. You're helping yourself. You even said you don't want to fend me off or look over your shoulder for the rest of your eternal life."

He chuckled. "Interesting take. I say after your mother and sister are safe on Feyrion you give me a little crossbow demonstration and maybe even a lesson or two. I want to see what I would have been up against had you gone through with the plan to kill me."

"Aren't you afraid I might turn my bow on you and make you bleed?"

Without warning, he disappeared. His chair moved. What the hell? Then she felt pressure on her shoulders, but it disappeared quickly. The chair returned to its original position, and Bevon came into view. Only this time he was grinning. "That was to show you that even if you shot your crossbow, I'm fast enough to either catch it or get out of the way. And if I disappear on you, I'll be hard to hit."

Zulema wasn't sure what to say. "I guess I should say thank you for joining forces with me. My question is why wasn't Derrick Valoric aware of your talents?"

"Derrick Valoric. Oh, yes. I never understood what my cousin saw in him. She claims they were mates."

"Why do you doubt it?" Zulema didn't want to say that she was feeling this extremely odd attraction to him too.

That's because he's your mate, her dragon proclaimed. *I never thought you to be so oblivious.*

Zulema nearly jumped. Her inner dragon hadn't said anything in a very long time. And the first thing out of her mouth is a lie? Or was it?

I heard that, her animal said. *I am not lying. You feel it. I know, because I do too.*

Zulema had other things to think about than the hot man in front of her. *Let me get my mother and sister to safety and we'll talk,* she shot back.

Denial is an ugly trait.

Since when did her dragon become so cynical?

Bevon reached across the table and cupped her hand. "Are you okay?"

Zulema never lost focus like that. "Yes. I'm fine."

"Where did you go?"

Shit. "Just going over the plan in my mind."

His brows rose. "It looked like you were arguing with someone. Your dragon perhaps?"

She stiffened. "How do you know about…"

"About your inner dragon? My brother's mate is a dragon shifter."

Ah, yes. Tory Sinclair. "My animal was asking if I was right in trusting you."

"Sure, she was."

Zulema wanted to redirect the focus to him. Besides, the more she understood his abilities the better. "Do you have any kind of inner voice?"

"Are you asking if I have a conscience?"

"I suppose that is what it is called."

He shook his head. "Nothing out of the ordinary."

"I see."

"Trying to understand my family is futile though. I've yet to truly know what my sisters are capable of. They even creep me out sometimes."

Zulema couldn't help but smile. "Good to know."

As if they could read each other's minds, they finished their meals. Her appetite wasn't the best, in part because she was worried this plan might go wrong, but she ate anyway. Zulema needed her strength.

When they finished, Bevon paid, for which she was thankful.

"Ready?" he asked.

She inhaled. "Yes."

Once they were outside, he turned to her. "We'll cut through this back alley, so we can teleport without curious eyes."

Zulema stepped close and grabbed his arm. A split second later, they were standing behind the nursing home.

"Nice," he said.

"What? Didn't you think my teleporting skills would be accurate?"

"Just saying it was nice. Nothing more." He had that cute little smirk. Always with the smirk, though she had to say, it was rather charming.

Maybe she was a bit jumpy. "Let's free Mom."

Inside, she signed in. "It's after visiting hours," the desk person said.

"I've been out of town, and I just need to check up on her. We'll be quick." Really? Ruth had seen her come and go over the last year every few days.

Ruth hesitated. "Your friend needs to sign in too."

"No problem." We both added our signatures to the roster. "We're good?"

"Yes, but don't stay long, and please, try not to draw much attention."

What was that supposed to mean? Zulema never caused a stir. "We won't."

Zulema took off with Bevon on her heals. When they reached the nurse's station on her mother's floor, she slipped an arm in Bevon's. She wanted it to appear as if they were a couple. The main nurse knew all of the residents' visitors.

"Zulema," the night nurse said. "We've missed you."

She'd only been gone a few days. "I've been busy." She looked up at Bevon, pretending as if they were in love. When the idea didn't offend her, she dismissed that fanciful notion to nerves.

"I see," the woman said with a grin.

"Actually, I've been away in part because I learned my mother is in danger of being killed."

The nurse sucked in a breath. "From whom?"

Zulema didn't need to get into it. "From a group who call themselves the Zon. It's why Bevon and I are going to take her someplace safe. I didn't want you to worry when you find her missing the next time you do rounds."

"Your mother can't be moved. Her health is too fragile."

Zulema figured the woman would claim that. "We'll take that chance."

"Where are you going?"

Zulema had expected that question too. "It will be better if you don't know."

Not wanting to answer any more questions, she and Bevon headed to her mother's room. When they entered, she was pleased to see that no one was there. Zulema turned to Bevon. "I'll let you take it from here."

He looked at the equipment her mom was hooked up to. "Don't worry. She won't be needing any of this medication."

"If your mother can see to my mom right away, we can also leave the oxygen behind too."

He looked to the side as if he was telepathing with his mother and nodded. He turned back to her. "My mother is ready. Go ahead and unhook her.

To Zulema's surprise, her mother didn't wake up during the process. Her breathing was a bit raspy, but that wasn't anything new. Once they freed her, Bevon stood on one side and Zulema on the other. "I'll teleport us to behind the facility. Then you can create the portal."

Bevon flashed her a quick smile. "I can do that. You know, we make a good team."

Zulema couldn't think about that. "Ready?"

"You're in denial. I'll have to work on changing that."

Not wanting anything to do with Bevon and his smug attitude right now, she teleported the three of them to the back of the nursing home. Together, they placed her mom on the grass. The cool air must have revived her, because her mother opened her eyes.

Zulema dropped to her knees. "It's okay, Mom. We're moving you to a place where you can get better."

"Zulema?" She reached out, and Zulema grasped her hand.

"Yes, it's me." She looked up at Bevon. "Any time now."

"Sorry." He stepped to the side, swung his arms in a circle, and out of nowhere a portal appeared. Bevon stepped back to them, squatted down, and lifted her mother as if she weighed nothing. He rose and walked to the portal. "You coming?"

Like she'd let him take her mother by himself. Zulema rose and jogged after him. They stepped through the portal. Instantly, the warm, clean air, wrapped its comforting arms around her.

Bevon turned to her. "Hold on. We'll teleport to my house."

Zulema took hold of her mother's hand so that the three of them were connected.

"My mom just telepathed that we should take your mother to the blue room."

Keeping a hold on her mother, the three teleported once more. Only after Bevon placed her mother on the bed, did Zulema let go. His mother appeared next to the bed. "Why don't you two grab something to eat while I do my magic."

Zulema wasn't so sure that she wanted to leave her mother alone with this woman, but Bevon's mom did seem to be powerful enough to do whatever she wanted.

Bevon placed a hand on Zulema's back. "Come on."

"Okay." They didn't need to eat, but clearly his mother wanted to be alone.

A second later, they appeared in the kitchen. The teleporting without warning was becoming rather disorienting. Not having had the chance to look around his parents' home before, she checked it out. The kitchen was huge. And it had three chefs. Three!

"Master Bevon, it's nice to see you back so soon," said a rather elderly plump woman.

"Nice to be back. I miss your cooking." He turned to Zulema. "What would you like to eat?"

"We just had dinner, but I could use a glass of wine."

Bevon rattled off a brand she'd never heard of. "Let's sit in the drawing room. They'll bring it to us."

"On second thought, as much as I would like some wine, May-lora will be rather frantic. I told her we would come for her a little after ten."

"One glass, and then we'll rescue her."

"Maybe we should go now," Zulema said.

"Give my mother a few more minutes. You'll feel better knowing that your mom has improved."

"What can she do in only a few minutes?"

He chuckled. "Oh, ye of little faith." Bevon glanced downward and then nodded.

She knew the signs. He was telepathing his mother. "What did she say?"

He smiled. "You're learning my tells, I see. Your mother is asking for you."

Zulema's heart dropped to her stomach. "Is my mom okay?"

Bevon stood and held out his hand. "See for yourself."

Since she had no idea where the blue room was in relation to where they were, she clasped his hand. A moment later, she was looking at her mother, who was sitting up in bed. Her color had returned, and her breathing wasn't labored. "Mom?"

"Zulema. This wonderful woman has brought me back from the brink of death."

Zulema looked over at Queen Arianna. "How?"

"I'm a Fairy, my dear. I'm happy to have helped. Your mother needs her rest now though. Tomorrow perhaps, she'll want to go outside and explore the garden."

An overwhelming sense of relief and wonder filled her. If this woman hadn't been a queen, Zulema might have hugged her. "I can't thank you enough."

"As long as you don't try to kill my son, it will be repayment enough."

"I promise."

Bevon placed a hand on Zulema's back, and his touch elicited something inside of her she wasn't ready to address—at least not until Maylora was safe. She turned back to her mother. "Bevon and I are going to bring Maylora here."

"That would be wonderful."

The wine would have to wait. They teleported outside. "I'll create the portal. Once we're in Tarradon, I'll let you take us to your sister's."

Gratitude overwhelmed her. She turned around, stood on her toes, and kissed him on the cheek. It had meant to be casual, but her body betrayed her. Zulema cleared her throat. "Sorry."

The right side of his mouth turned up. "For what? I rather enjoyed it. Anytime you want to continue, I'm happy to oblige."

His cavalier attitude made her laugh. "You are something else, Bevon Forrester. Now please make a portal."

He did so, and they portaled to his house. "Let's save Maylora."

Zulema grabbed his hand and teleported into her sister's living room. The lights were off, and even though it was close to eleven, Zulema was a little surprised that her sister wasn't waiting up for her. When she spotted her pink suitcase near the front door, Zulema relaxed a bit. Instead of teleporting to the bedroom, she raced up the steps, making enough noise to rouse the dead. "Maylora?"

Her sister's bedroom door was wide open, and a trickle of dread filled her. She rushed in and flipped on the light. Shit. Her sister's bed was still made. Wanting to be thorough, she checked the bathroom. Where was she?

Zulema rushed downstairs, hoping her sister was hiding somewhere. She called out again but received no answer.

"You didn't find her?" Bevon asked.

"No. Her suitcase is by the door, so she was ready for us."

Bevon walked over to the front door and ran a hand down the edge. "The door has been forced open."

Zulema's knees weakened. "Oh, shit. I bet Derrick Valoric took her."

Bevon rushed over to her and clasped her shoulders. "Don't worry. We'll find her."

"How?"

"We'll make him come to us."

"You think he will?"

"I have my ways. Now, how about returning to my cabin to brainstorm our next move?"

"Let's go."

Chapter Ten

BEVON HAD NEVER felt this helpless before, mainly because his powers were so strong. This time was different. A lot was at stake, and he didn't have a plan. Lure Derrick to them? What had he been thinking? He hoped that between him and Zulema, they would be able to figure something out.

While it was hard to believe the universe would do this to him, the more time he spent with Zulema, the more he was ready to accept that she was his mate. How ironic was that? The woman had been on a mission to kill him. What kind of gods did that to a person? Right now, he had to push aside his desires and concentrate on finding her sister.

"Tell me again where you were when you were captured." Bevon had teleported them back to his place so they wouldn't be disturbed. Not only that, being in her sister's house appeared to distract Zulema.

"Why does it matter now?" Zulema asked, sounding both defiant and a bit defeated.

"It might give me a clue as to Derrick's abilities."

She exhaled. "Fine. All I remember was that I was in town at a bar. I left by the back entrance so I could teleport home. Someone must have drugged me, because the next thing I knew, I was waking up in a cell with my ankles and wrists chained to the floor."

His fists clenched. "Dear goddess."

"Tell me about it. I tried to teleport, but Derrick somehow had managed to block my powers."

Bevon paced. "That means he could have teleported you anywhere. It also means he's quite powerful if he was able to block your ability to teleport."

"And shoot fire from my hands."

He couldn't imagine the horror of losing so much of her identity all at once. "Did you at any time try to shift?"

"No, the ceiling was too low."

He nodded. "I wonder how he knew you could teleport. It's rare for a dragon shifter to have that ability."

"That's true, but he said he'd been watching me. It was why he picked me to kill you—or rather try to kill you."

"That's wrong on so many levels. What else do you remember? Even the smallest detail might prove beneficial." He grabbed two beers from the refrigerator. "Want one?" he asked.

"Absolutely."

He liked a woman who didn't mind a man's drink. "If Derrick gave you an assignment, he must have told you how to contact him once you killed me."

She snapped her fingers and then pulled out a medallion from her inside pocket. "Yes. Tamarella gave this to Derrick so he could create a portal to Feyrion. He then gave it to me since he knew I'd have to go to there for the treniam. He also said I could use it to contact him."

"So that's how you made it to my home world without my knowledge. May I ask where you landed?"

"Some place high on a mountain overlooking a lake."

"We have many such locations, but it was smart of Tamarella to have him land away from town," he said. "Until we figure out a few things, let's not contact Derrick."

"I too want to have a plan in place before we do. If we rush in without much thought, he could kill Maylora."

Her level-headed approach impressed him. "I imagine if Derrick ever decides to kill your sister, he will contact you first to demand that you speed up your mission." At least he hoped that was true. If anything happened to Zulema's sister though, it would devastate her.

"He gave me two weeks. I'm hoping he honors that timeline."

"An honorable man would." The only thing that gave him hope was that Tamarella seemed to desire Derrick. He couldn't be all that bad.

Zulema tossed back her beer and nodded. "Your sister knew about my mother's illness. Do you think she might know something about the whereabouts of Maylora?"

Bevon smiled. "You are good. I will ask her."

"Sweet sisters. I need your help. Could you join me and my mate at my house?" He figured the mention of his mate would get them there. *"But whatever you do, don't mention…"* Before he could finish his sentence both of his sisters appeared. *"I was about to say, don't mention that she is my mate. We have not discussed it yet."*

Neither of his sisters even glanced his way or acknowledged his request. Instead, they rushed over to Zulema. Oh, boy.

"Nice to see you again, Zulema. I have to admit, this is a bit of a surprise," Fay said.

"For me, too. I trust your brother filled you in?"

Fay looked over at Bevon. "Not exactly. Bevon is not the overly sharing type."

"I share," he said.

Meena laughed. She turned to Zulema and introduced herself. "I imagine you've heard of Tally, our sister who prefers Feyrion to here?"

"Yes, but I don't believe I've met her."

He needed to intervene. "We weren't at home for long." Since he wanted their help, he motioned they all take a seat. Bevon then detailed everything he could. "Now that Zulema's sister is missing, we need help finding her."

"Are you sure that Valoric—or rather the Zon—took her?" Meena asked.

"Almost positive," Zulema chimed in. "I spoke with Maylora earlier in the day and outlined the danger she was in. Her suitcase was by the door when Bevon and I arrived. To me, that implied she was ready and waiting for me to take her to safety, so it stands to reason that the Zon intervened."

"I'm sorry," Fay said. "We'll find her."

"How? The Zon could have taken her anywhere."

Fay smiled. "Leave that to us. Do you have anything that belongs to your sister?"

"Not with me, but I can get something. Are you saying you can touch someone's belongings and learn about their whereabouts?" she asked.

"Usually—when Meena and I combine our talents."

"Since when?" Bevon asked.

"Brother, brother. This is what happens when you don't pay attention. Your sisters can achieve a lot when we work together. You and Kenton should try it."

He didn't think a Fey's powers worked that way.

Zulema stood. "I'll retrieve my sister's suitcase. Once we find her, she'll need it anyway."

The idea that the Zon might be watching troubled him. "I'll go instead."

Before Zulema had the chance to argue with him, he teleported to Maylora's house. If the Zon were watching or tracking her, the less they saw of her the better. At least his home was immune to all tracking.

Once in her sister's house, he grabbed the suitcase and returned. "Here it is."

"I was going to go," Zulema said.

"I know, but who's to say the Zon aren't watching your sister's house."

"Do you think they are?" she asked. "Dumb question. They've already taken her, but they wouldn't want to harm me until I've killed you."

Bevon didn't like the quick shot of fear in her eyes—or perhaps it was anger. He held out his hand. "May I see the portal device. I'm hoping there isn't a tracking device on it."

Zulema's mouth opened. "Oh, shit. I didn't think of that."

As soon as she gave it to him, he handed it to Fay. "What can you tell me about this?"

Fay held it in her palm and closed her eyes. "I'm feeling evil."

That wasn't a surprise. "Can you tell the location of its origin?"

"Not precisely, but it's somewhere on the west side of Avonbelle."

"That's where I live," Zulema said. She turned to Bevon. "I should have thought to ask Tamarella's handmaiden where Derrick lives."

"I'll contact Tally and ask her to check," Bevon said.

"Is everything okay?" his third sister asked.

He explained the need to ask Betina if Tamarella ever mentioned where she met up with Derrick Valoric when she visited.

"I can ask, but I believe she's retired for the night."

"Wake her. A woman's life might be on the line."

"Okay."

"Tally is asking Betina," he told Zulema.

"Thank you." She placed a hand on his arm, and lust shot up his spine. Whoa. That reaction was unexpected but not surprising. She was his mate after all, but if they were going to save Maylora, he needed to shut down his urges. "When you picked up the suitcase, did you sense anyone watching the house? Or could they have installed some kind of security system to watch my sister's comings and goings? I don't want to believe they are all-knowing."

That was a disturbing thought. "I didn't, but I will check. His mind had been too focused on other things. *"Kenton, you up for a little reconnaissance?"* he telepathed.

"Now?" his brother shot back.

"Yes. Zulema's sister was kidnapped. I think the Zon might have been watching her sister's home, which was how they knew when to grab her." It didn't matter that Zulema had called her. They could have tapped his mate's phone.

"Be right there, just as soon as I speak with Tory."

Bevon was a little jealous at how well his brother and his mate—the future queen of Feyrion—shared things.

A few seconds later, both Kenton and Tory appeared. Both were flushed, as if they'd been engaging in some fun activity. "Sorry to disturb you two," Bevon said, a bit embarrassed.

"No problem." Kenton turned to Zulema and introduced himself and his mate.

"It's nice to finally meet you both, though I apologize for you even having to be here."

Kenton held up his hand. "We understand. Bevon explained why you were sent, and I'm sorry you were put in such a situation."

Bevon turned to the side. *"Betina doesn't know where Valoric lives, other than it was in Avonbelle Province,"* Tally telepathed to all but Zulema.

"Thanks." He faced his mate. "Betina has no idea where Valoric lives."

"Oh."

Kenton placed a hand on Bevon's arm. "Ready to check out Zulema's sister's home?"

"Yes, but let's cloak ourselves until we know what we're up against. And Zulema?"

"Yes."

"I'd like you to stay here. I don't trust Valoric."

"No way."

"You're safe here. We won't be long. No telling if he's tracking you. I'm guessing it's either with the medallion or your phone. He could have listened in."

Her shoulders sagged. "That bastard."

Bevon wanted to hug her, but he doubted she'd appreciate it. "We won't be long."

Kenton held Tory's hand and placed his other hand on Bevon's shoulder. A second later they were outside of Maylora's house. For the next few minutes, they searched around the outside of the house. He could sense a trail of someone who'd been there.

"Let's go inside," Bevon said.

The three teleported to the living room. He turned on the light, in part to see if the Zon would suddenly come out of the woodwork. Thankfully, they didn't, though it was possible they were aware of the new arrivals.

"They had to have known Zulema's sister was about to leave since they'd done nothing for days," Bevon said. "Unless they tapped her phone."

"Or there could be a surveillance system."

"All the more reason to telepath," Tory said.

Bevon should have thought of that. *"Good point."*

Like a well-oiled team, they spread out and searched, looking for any cameras, recording devices, and the such.

Ten minutes later, Tory called to them. *"Found something."*

He and Kenton located her on her knees by the front door. Tory lifted the entrance mat to expose a small plate. How simple. "I'm guessing that when someone steps on it, it sends a signal to their headquarters—or directly to Derrick's house." Bevon spoke out loud, not seeing the need to telepath anymore.

"Agreed," his brother said. "I wonder if we can find where the signal is coming from."

"I don't have that talent," Bevon said.

"We should ask my cousin, Logan. Or better yet, his brother Camden. I bet he's designed stuff like this before," Tory said.

He liked that idea. "How about taking a picture of it and asking one or both of them to check it out? If you remove it, Derrick might notice it and harm Zulema's sister in retaliation."

"Sounds good," Kenton said. "Tory and I will head back and ask for Camden's help. Let's hope our sisters can be more productive."

"Let's hope. And thanks. Tell Camden I'll stop by tomorrow with a portal device Derrick gave Zulema. I'm thinking it might also have a tracking device inside it. That, or the Zon have eyes and ears everywhere."

"Will do." Kenton squeezed Bevon's shoulder. "Just remember

to treat your mate well."

"How did you—?"

Kenton grinned, and then he and Tory disappeared. His two sisters must have spilled the beans. Nothing was sacred anymore. He teleported back to the woods.

Zulema jumped up. "Well?"

He told them what they'd found, and that Tory would try to find more information on the transmitting device located under the welcome mat.

"Bastard. Now what?" Zulema asked.

"Unless my two lovely sisters here have a plan, I don't see what more we can do tonight."

Meena smiled. "We believe we know where Maylora is."

"Why didn't you tell me?" Zulema said.

"What would you have done if they had?" Bevon said. "Knowing how stubborn you can be, you would have gone after her—without me."

She huffed out a breath. "Maybe."

He loved her spunk. "Where is she?" he asked his sisters.

"We'll show you. It will be faster than explaining where she is. We don't do addresses very well," Fay said.

Bevon faced Zulema. He wanted to tell her to stay put, but he didn't think she'd listen. "You can come with us, but how about we go in cloaked, assess the situation, and then regroup? This is not a snatch and grab mission. We don't need him to retaliate if we do."

Her face scrunched up for a second, and then she let out a breath. "If I know Maylora is okay, I can wait a bit longer."

That was a relief. "Good. Make sure you don't do anything rash." Bevon smiled so as not to piss her off.

"I have a question for you, brother," Fay said.

"Yes?"

"Suppose you eventually save Maylora. Valoric will assume Zulema is no longer planning to kill you, which means he'll send someone else to carry out his mission."

"Let him," Bevon shot back.

"What if he sends someone to kill Zulema instead? She's not as powerful as we are."

"Shit." He faced his mate. "She's right. I'm all for making sure that your sister is okay, but let's make sure we save her after you kill me."

Chapter Eleven

WHAT WAS BEVON talking about? "I couldn't kill you even if I tried."

He chuckled. "I wasn't being literal, but I'm hoping you don't want me dead."

The time for playing the tough warrior was over. As much as Zulema didn't want to admit it, the only way this mission was going to end well was if she was honest. Besides, Bevon had proven that he wanted to help. "I don't."

Bevon smiled. "Good. I meant that we should play act at killing me. You can pretend to run some treniam down my arm, I'll fall to the ground, and then you take out your arrow and shoot me."

"No! You'll bleed." Bevon clearly didn't understand what an arrow to the heart at close range would do to a person.

"I'll wear protective gear, princess."

"Oh. And then what? You'll lie on the ground for a week or so? It's possible that Derrick will send someone to confirm you're dead. So what if he said the Zon is supposed to be everywhere. He probably said that just to scare me."

Bevon shook his head. "I'm hoping he knows that when a Fey royalty dies, his relatives take his or her body into their home—or estate as the case may be. There will be a small viewing on Feyrion followed by a burial. That's what happened when Tamarella died. As I am lying on the ground *dying*, I'll telepath to my sisters to help me. They will rush out and immediately teleport me to Feyrion. I'll work something out from there."

She thought about it for a moment. "I guess that could work.

Even if Derrick insists on seeing for himself that you're dead and manages to reach Feyrion, he can't get into your house, unless he can teleport inside, right?"

Bevon shook his head. "Not even then. We have what I would call a magic shield around the property. A person has to be accepted before we allow him in. Trust me, Derrick Valoric will not be allowed anywhere near us."

The plan had merit. "How about we make sure that Maylora is safe first?" Zulema asked. "Then I'll worry about what happens next."

"That works. I just wanted you to understand Maylora's role in the big scheme of things." He turned to his sisters. "Ready, ladies, to guide us to Zulema's sister?"

"Of course."

Bevon grabbed Zulema's hand, surprising her in its strength and comfort. Only at the last second did she remember that she needed to cloak herself once they arrived. When they made it to their destination, she was sure they were at the wrong place. In front of them was a rather large house. To be honest, she'd expected something a bit more sinister.

"You said you'd met Valoric, right?" she whispered.

"Once."

"Did you get the sense he lived in a place like this?"

"I only met him briefly, but yes. The man was arrogant enough to own a nice place—even if he couldn't afford it." He tapped her nose. "We should keep talking to a minimum, my warrior. The last thing we need is to alert any guards."

His comment stung, mostly because he was right. Zulema nodded.

He leaned in closer. "If you feel your cloaking is requiring too much energy, just hold onto me. My shield can cover both of us."

"Thank you," she whispered.

Zulema had a lot to learn about this man. Since she didn't see either of his sisters, she assumed they'd just been the guides and had returned to the forest.

With a hand to her back, he teleported them inside the dark home. She had no idea if anyone associated with the Zon lived here, let alone if her sister was being held in the home, but Zulema was game to look around. Since no one could see them, her sense of well-being remained intact.

Bevon kept her close to him. Because cloaking took effort, she let down her guard and used his powers to shield her. This Fey's abilities continued to impress her.

Bevon took them from room to room looking for Maylora. One such room had a man dressed in a uniform sitting at a desk. Whoops. When he didn't look up, she relaxed a bit.

She grabbed Bevon's arm to indicate they should leave. He immediately teleported them to what had to be the basement. It smelled of mold and some substance she couldn't identify. He led them toward a door that had been padlocked.

Zulema indicated she wanted to see what was inside. When Bevon teleported them, she froze at the sight. Her sister was asleep on a dirty cot with one arm chained to the wall. Zulema stepped away from Bevon and rushed over to her sister. "Maylora, wake up," she whispered. "It's me. Zulema."

Her sister groaned. When she opened her eyes, it seemed to take a moment for her to recognize who it was, possibly because it was so dark—or maybe because some ass had drugged her sister, just like he had Zulema.

"Zulema?" her sister croaked.

"Yes, it's me."

Maylora struggled to sit up. "Someone kidnapped me and drugged me."

Before Zulema could say anything or tell her she and Bevon would return for her, the door flew opened. "What the hell?" the guard said.

Damn. Just as she was about to cloak herself, Bevon grabbed her and pulled her to her feet. His touch made her invisible again, and a second later, they were back at his house.

"Why did we have to leave?" she said in not the nicest of tones. "I could have taken down the guard!"

"Were you willing to get caught? Again?"

"Of course not, but I would have cloaked myself. He wouldn't have been able to defend himself. I could have snatched the key to the chains." She didn't understand this man.

"We decided not to free your sister this go around."

"I know, but—"

"There is no but. Besides, can you be certain the man wouldn't have opened fire in the room? He did see you, although briefly."

Zulema hadn't even noticed if he was carrying a weapon or not. Shit. She was losing it. Even she had to admit that a quick spray of bullets would have wounded her, and possibly Bevon or even Maylora. The room was at most eight feet by eight feet. Being cloaked merely meant a person couldn't see her. They were still there. "I know. You're right. And to make matters worse, I've put my sister at risk of being killed. The guard will surely contact Derrick, who will know that I'm not following the plan. I say we go back and incapacitate the guy before he contacts Derrick." Or was it too late?

"He might have already called him, but to admit that someone got in the house without his notice might cause his head to roll. It's possible the guard will keep things to himself and move Maylora on his own. Regardless of the guard's response, I'll return to that house—alone—to make sure nothing happens to your sister. If he or anyone tries anything, they won't see the sunrise tomorrow. I'm anticipating your sister will be moved elsewhere now that the site has been compromised."

His logic was mostly sound. "Why wouldn't they just kill her if they know I've changed the plan?" Her pulse skyrocketed at that horrible thought.

"The guard might not know it was you. Not only was it dark in the small room, you were visible for less than two seconds. Even if he recognized you, and he contacted Valoric, Derrick would demand that you return to the original plan. For you to agree though, he'd need your sister alive."

"Let's hope you're right. Whatever the guard is planning though, I'm going with you."

Bevon cupped her shoulders. "What I'm saying is that you are vulnerable when it comes to your sister. You might let your emotions, rather than your logic, rule again."

Bevon acted as if he didn't think she was capable of handling herself. So what if that exact scenario had just occurred? "I would not, or at least I'd try to control myself this time."

Bevon crossed his arms. "Suppose you see the guards mistreat Maylora. Can you assure me you won't try to intervene?"

"Of course, I would."

"I rest my case," he said.

He wasn't the only one who could use logic. "Tell me this. If they move Maylora, what will you do?"

"I see what you're doing. You want to know if I'm concerned for your sister's safety. The answer is yes I am. That being said, could I take her to safety? I certainly could teleport her back to Feyrion, but the consequences might be more than you are willing or able to deal with."

"What consequences?"

"He could come after you, and I'm assuming you want this mess done and over with—just like I do."

If he didn't have a decent argument, she would have fought back. Without any leverage over her to kill Bevon, Derrick might decide just to kill her and have someone else carry out his plan. "Fine. Follow them. Tomorrow, I'll pretend to kill you, and then we'll save my sister."

"Deal." He moved in front of Zulema and kissed her quickly before she could react. "Be back when I can." The arrogant man grinned and then disappeared.

Zulema pressed her fingertips to her lips, not wanting to react, but she did. Her lips burned from the quick kiss, and her heart raced with excitement. She didn't like it one bit—or so she told herself.

Wahoo! her dragon said. *It's about time you two did what you've been aching to do.*

What are you talking about? Her dragon was out of control. Zulema assumed it was because Bevon was so powerful that her animal took his side.

He is our mate. The sooner you admit it, the sooner we can have some fun.

Are you crazy? I can't think about that now. We have to get Derrick Valoric off my back first, and for that to happen, I have to pretend to kill Bevon and then save Maylora. Then I'll figure out what to do about this crazy attraction.

Her dragon shot a hot blast into her stomach. *Remember what I said: denial is ugly.*

Stop saying that.

Zulema didn't have time for this. She paced his home, making sure she understood what needed to happen tomorrow. His cabin was small, but it was cozy and safe. However, because she had excess energy, she stepped outside for a breath of air. Stars peeked through parts of the heavy canopy, and the slightly cool temperature helped clear her head.

Just in case the Zon was watching her, Zulema cloaked herself and walked toward the eternal flame. She was tempted to follow Bevon to the house that she guessed was owned by Derrick. Only Zulema wouldn't. Bevon was right about one thing. If she saw anyone mistreating her sister, she'd attack him, and that could jeopardize her, her sister, and possibly her mother's well-being.

At some point, if her mother's health continued to improve, she wouldn't want to stay on Feyrion. She'd insist on returning home to Avonbelle Province to resume her life. Since her mother possessed few skills—other than what was imbued by all dragon shifters—she wouldn't be able to fend off several Zon members at once.

Zulema wouldn't be surprised if Derrick had guards or cameras positioned near her mother's home and near the nursing home just in case she returned—assuming he was aware she was gone.

There had to be something Zulema could do though. Someone must know where Derrick lived. His home—assuming it belonged to him—was near her home, or so Tamarella's maid had said.

Most likely Bevon would be gone for some time, giving her the opportunity to teleport to her town and make a few calls. Someone should be able to provide her with information about Derrick Valoric or his Zon organization.

Happy with that relatively safe solution, she left. The coffee shop where Zulema often went was still open. With her usual coffee in hand, Zulema found a booth and called a friend who was very talented when it came to doing research. Zulema's computer was at her house, and while she could have gone there to retrieve it, she didn't want to be seen anywhere near there. Most likely, the Zon was watching her place too.

Her friend answered. "Zulema! Where have you been?"

That was the big question. Aislin was aware of Zulema's body-guard job but not that she'd been ordered to kill a man. "I'm in trouble, or rather my sister is in trouble because of me."

"Oh, no."

"I need you to do me a favor."

"Anything," Aislin said.

Speaking softly, Zulema outlined what had happened in the last few days, leaving out the detail that Derrick's mate lived on a different realm or that Bevon was a Fey. "I need you to learn anything you can about Derrick Valoric and a woman named Anna DeLeon." The real Anna might have been to Valoric's home.

"I can do that. When do you need it by?"

"Now?"

Aislin laughed. "Give me an hour."

"You are the best."

"I have an idea. Why don't you come over? It will be easier in case I need some information."

Zulema couldn't say no to that offer. If her phone was tapped, she didn't need to be using it more than necessary. Shit. She'd totally forgotten about that possibility. "Be right there."

With her coffee in hand, she left the shop, worked her way to a side alley, and then teleported to her friend's house. Even though Aislin had seen her teleport hundreds of times, she always acted surprised when Zulema popped up out of nowhere. "That was fast."

"Teleporting always is," Zulema said.

Aislin tapped her computer. "Let's see what dirt I can dig up on this guy and your mysterious woman."

Chapter Twelve

WHEN BEVON RETURNED from watching the Zon move Maylora to a different location, he expected to see Zulema relaxing on the sofa, perhaps watching television. When he found the house empty, a wave of despair grabbed him.

"Zulema?" He didn't know why he called her name. Perhaps he thought she might be out back getting a breath of fresh air and would hear him.

Just to be thorough, he checked out back but didn't detect her. *"Fay or Meena. Have either of you seen Zulema?"* He didn't want to panic, but he couldn't help it.

"No," they telepathed in unison.

Damn it. She hadn't gone to the original house where her sister had been held. He'd been there for hours and never sensed her. Could she have gone home in need of something? The fastest way to find out would have been to teleport to Zulema's house. The only problem was he didn't know where she lived—only where her sister did. Zulema probably wouldn't have gone to the hotel in Edendale because she said she'd already packed up her stuff. There was no use paying for a room she wasn't going to use, and he had agreed with her.

"Zulema, where are you?" he mumbled.

Bevon refused to believe that Valoric had found her. Bevon's home was invisible to all but those he wanted to have the sight. Frustrated, he teleported next door to where his sisters lived. Neither were in the living room, which meant they were in bed. *"Sorry to disturb you, but I need help finding Zulema."*

A few seconds later, both of his sisters appeared. "Do you think she went to save her sister?"

"No." He explained that he'd just been there. "I'm thinking maybe she went home, only I don't know where that is."

"What you need is a locator bracelet like the one I made for our brother and Tory."

"You're right, but I need to find Zulema first in order to give it to her."

Fay smiled. "I'll make one for you tomorrow."

"Thank you. Any idea where she might live?"

His two sisters faced each other and then held hands. In silence, they joined their magic, and Bevon knew better than to interfere. Two long minutes later they opened their eyes. Fay smiled. "I believe if you return to your house, you will find her."

"I was just there." She dipped her chin, indicating there was no use arguing with her. "Fine."

When he teleported next door, to his intense delight, Zulema was in the kitchen pouring herself a glass of water. He rushed over to her and had to touch her to make sure she was real. "Where have you been? I was worried."

Before he let her respond, he grabbed her to his chest and hugged her. The warmth and comfort confirmed once more that she was indeed his mate—not that he had any doubt. When she leaned back, he tried not to show his disappointment. He'd never been with a woman who didn't want to be with him, but he understood her hesitation. His logic about how to do things didn't always align with her desires.

"I didn't know how long you'd be gone. Since I wanted to find more information on Valoric and Tamarella's friend, Anna DeLeon, I contacted my friend, Aislin, who is a very talented computer person. I thought she could do a deep dive for me."

Bevon exhaled. "That was smart. Join me on the sofa. We need to talk."

He walked over to the living room while Zulema followed. He

would have grabbed a beer, but he wanted her to understand this was serious and not a drinking matter.

Zulema sat on the chair across from the sofa instead of next to him. Bevon wished he understood why she was so adverse to him. "Before you begin, could I ask you to do me a favor?" he asked.

"What is it?"

"When I returned home and found you gone, I panicked."

She sucked in a breath. "I'm sorry. I thought I would be home before you."

Arguing would do him no good. "Okay, but maybe leave a note next time?"

She smiled. "I can do that."

He'd bring up the locator bracelet that would allow them to communicate tomorrow. "Tell me what you learned."

"You first. Did they move my sister?"

"Yes, to another nice home a few miles away."

"How did she seem?" Zulema asked.

"You sister was awake and walking. Does she have any powers?"

"She's a dragon shifter so she can fly and shoot fire, but she can't teleport or cloak herself. I imagine Derrick, or whoever took her, blocked her ability to shift, which means she's basically helpless."

That would be smart on Derrick's part. "As soon as you pretend to kill me, I imagine Derrick will return your sister. I agree that this plan needs to take place tomorrow."

She sighed. "That would be great. Maylora isn't tough, and this incarceration will crush her for years to come."

He shook his head. "How did two sisters end up so different?" Though he could ask himself the same question. He and Kenton were quite different too. Zulema sucked in her bottom lip, and Bevon's thoughts raced to something rather erotic.

"I'm five years older than my sister. My dad, who was a warlock, died when she was six. My mother's health deteriorated a few years after that, and I had no choice but to take the role of provider and protector."

He whistled. "That's a big burden for someone so young."

She shrugged. "It wasn't as if I had much of a choice."

He patted the seat next to him. "Come here." He held his breath, hoping she would join him on the sofa.

Zulema's mouth twisted right and then left before she stood and moved. It took all of Bevon's control not to hug and kiss her. "Tell me what you found out about Derrick Valoric." He assumed she thought this Anna DeLeon might know where Derrick lived.

"Not much. Aislin found a house that Derrick bought a few years back, but she couldn't tell if he still lives there. It's close to where my sister was held captive the first time though. Since it was growing late, I thought I'd stop by Anna's house tomorrow and ask her if she knows where he lives."

"Do you have that address of Derrick's property? Your sister was moved about three miles from the first house."

She rattled off the address. "That means she's not at his home. Derrick's property is more like ten miles away."

"It's good intel though," he said. "It might come in useful in the future if he moves her again. It would be a shame to mount a rescue only to find she wasn't there. I'd like to be sure he didn't sell the place to someone else." He tapped his thigh. "I have an idea."

"What is it?" she asked.

"I need to talk with my computer expert. Give me a second. Be right back."

Even though it was late, Logan Caspian, who was Tory's cousin, would understand the need for immediacy. Bevon teleported to Logan's house. His home was dark, but Bevon sensed the presence of two people. Most likely it was Logan and his mate, Wendy. Bevon walked to the bedroom and tapped on the door. "It's me, Bevon."

A moment later, Logan came out. His pajama bottoms were on inside out, but Bevon appreciated the effort. "Is Tory okay?"

"Yes, she's fine. This is about Zulema."

Logan slipped out of his room. "Let's go into my office. What exactly do you need to know?"

Bevon gave him the address. "Can you tell me if a Derrick Valoric lives there?"

He booted up his computer, and it took Logan less than four minutes to find the answer. "No, he doesn't."

"Can you find his current address?"

"I'll try."

He tapped a few more keys. "I got lucky. I'll email you the address."

"You are the best," Bevon said.

"Who exactly is this Valoric character?"

"He hired Zulema to kill me."

Needless to say, Logan's eyes widened. "Talk about an impossible chore—unless she found some treniam."

"She didn't. Valoric thinks I killed his mate, who happens to be my cousin."

"I see."

As much as Bevon would have appreciated Logan's unbiased viewpoint, not only did Bevon not want to keep him, he needed to get back to Zulema. Even though his house was cloaked, he didn't trust Zulema not to wander off again. He stood. "I owe you one."

"Anytime."

Bevon teleported back to his house, and thankfully Zulema was still there. Instead of looking relieved he'd returned, she was pacing. He rushed up to her. Waves of concern and fear were washing off her. "What's wrong?"

"Derrick contacted me."

His blood pressure spiked. "How?"

She pulled the medallion from her pocket. "He used this." Zulema pressed the crystal and Valoric's voice sounded. "Shame on you, Zulema, for taking your mother. But don't worry, I found a replacement—a nice young lady named Aislin. If you ever want to see her alive, kill Forrester. Time is ticking."

When she looked up at him with such despair, all Bevon could do was reach out and pull her close. "Don't worry, we'll get both of them back."

He expected her to pull away like she had before, but instead, Zulema wrapped her arms around his waist, and a sense of well-being and security overwhelmed him. Bevon wasn't sure what came over him, but he leaned back, lifted her chin, and kissed her.

EVERY INSTINCT IN the world told Zulema to pull away, but no force existed that would make her move out of his grasp. Bevon was competent, secure, and everything she wanted in a man. Never before had she let herself feel so strongly about a person. Sure, her dragon kept saying he was her mate, but she found it hard to believe that she'd be lucky enough for the gods to pair them together.

Her dragon mother was mated to a warlock, and that combination was unconventional, but never in her wildest dreams did she think she'd get a Fey—and a prince at that!

Kiss him back, stupid, her dragon said, awakening from what seemed like a deep slumber.

Why not? Zulema wanted to experience what he had to offer and begged for entrance. Bevon obliged. One second they were standing in the living room and the next they were on a bed—his bed—with him lying next to her.

He dragged a knuckle down her cheek and smiled. "You do something to me that no other woman has ever come close to doing."

His words scorched a path of desire straight to her core. "Is that so?"

Zulema rarely flirted, mostly because there wasn't time in her life to do so, but with Bevon, it came naturally. Did she feel guilty about enjoying him while her friend and sister were being held captive? Hell yes, but even if they freed one or both of them, Derrick Valoric would find more people to take their place. His treachery would never end.

"Yes, that is so, but if you want to stop, tell me."

For once in her life, she decided to do something she wanted to do. "I'll be sure to keep that in mind."

Zulema cupped his face, causing streaks of pleasure to shoot through her. This whole sexual draw was totally unexpected but oh so pleasant.

He pulled her close and deepened the kiss, convincing her that Bevon must be sending magic through her body, because every touch and every taste altered her. Bevon let her in, and when their tongues collided, she knew without a doubt that they were indeed meant for each other. She hadn't planned to groan, but the delightful rush of lust was too much to deny.

Not being one to shy away from anything, she slipped a hand under his shirt and ran her palm up his muscled back. She broke the kiss to draw in a deep breath. "Oh, my."

He grinned. "Tit for tat?"

It was a phrase she'd never heard before. "Meaning?"

"I'll take off my shirt if you do the same."

Zulema laughed. No man had bothered to ask before. He just did it, but she liked the respect of him asking. "Deal, but let me do the honors."

His brows rose. "A tease, I see."

"I'm not teasing." Zulema rose to her knees and motioned for Bevon to sit up.

Once he did as she asked, she slowly lifted the material up over his stomach and then stopped when it revealed a body worthy of staring at. "Do you have to work at this physique?"

"Stay around long enough, and you'll find out."

So that was how it was going to be. That was okay. Zulema was up for the challenge.

Chapter Thirteen

Z ULEMA RELEASED HER hold on Bevon's shirt and removed hers. His pulse soared. He might have been mystified by his reason at one point about his attraction, but he wasn't any longer. While he didn't plan on living on Feyrion, he hoped Zulema wouldn't be against visiting his home world—as his princess. But that conversation would have to be put on hold. He had more important things to do. Like kiss her and make love to her.

Zulema exposed a feminine black lacy bra. Oh, my. Bevon had misjudged his little assassin. "Sweet."

He leaned closer when she held up a hand. "Your turn."

Fair was fair. Instead of using magic, he pulled up his shirt as slowly as he could. It was all about the reveal—or so women always claimed. When her eyes turned purple, pride rushed through him, until he noticed a white aura around his own arms and body, something that had never happened to him before. He'd been told it was the definitive sign that he and Zulema were meant to be.

"You're kind of glowing," Zulema said with awe in her voice. She slid a finger down his arm, probably to see if it was hot to the touch.

At some point he'd let her know what it meant, but now wasn't the time for the mate discussion. "It means I'm highly attracted to you."

"Is that so?"

"You can't deny you don't feel the same. Your eyes changed to purple." His heart pounded as he awaited her response.

"I won't deny I'm turned on." Zulema ran a hand down his

chest, her fingers leaving a scorching path of desire.

"But you're wondering if there is more, right?" Damn. Why did he say that? It had been stupid to bring up the topic, but he wanted to assure her that he wanted her wholeheartedly.

"Hmm. I can't be sure. Perhaps you can convince me." When she smiled, his cock nearly exploded.

"Just you wait." One minute she was on her knees, and the next she was flat on her back.

"Oh, my. I like a man who takes charge."

He hadn't expected that comment. Despite her claim that she liked a strong man, the kiss he bestowed was gentle yet passionate. Once he tasted her, however, Bevon wasn't sure if he could hold back from taking her. His blood heated, and his cock turned to steel. Never before had he needed to force himself to slow down.

Zulema opened her mouth and invited him in. That one action made his blood heat up further. His white glow intensified as he plunged his tongue into her mouth. In equal partnership, they explored and thrust, making a deep connection between them.

As much as he wanted to kiss her for hours, there were so many other places he had to touch and taste. Bevon swiped a hand and removed her bra. Ah, much better. He then slid lower, captured a delicate nipple in his mouth, and then sucked on the tiny nub. He loved how she drew in a sharp breath and then grabbed his shoulders, responding as if the desire was overwhelming her.

Wanting to take her higher, Bevon cupped her other breast and pinched the tip. Her moan came out loud. A moment later, she wrapped her legs around his waist.

He rolled to the side. "I need you naked, princess."

Without asking for his help, she kicked off her shoes and tugged down her jeans, taking her panties with them. Her desperation spoke volumes. The controlled Zulema Garcia would never engage in this kind of sex unless she believed he was innocent of murder—and that knowledge unlocked any inhibition he might have experienced.

Because he was in a hurry, Bevon swept a hand down his body, divesting himself of his clothes.

She smiled. "That's cheating."

He laughed. "Are you complaining?"

"Not in the least. Maybe next time, you can help me out."

Bevon grinned. Who knew this sassy woman existed under that tough exterior? "Promise."

Without further ado, he slid down between her legs, grabbed hold, and widened them. She returned her hands to his shoulders and dropped her head back. The first lick sent spikes of need through him so great, Bevon had to force his pulse to slow down. Shit, she was hot.

He continued his sensual assault, with his cock growing harder and harder until he was forced to stop or come. Bevon rolled onto his back and pulled Zulema on top of him. Her lips were slightly swollen and her eyes a bit glassy.

"My turn," she said.

That hadn't been his plan—it had been for her to ride him. Before he could stop her though, she lifted onto her knees and slid toward his feet until her lips were at his cock. Fearing he might press too hard if he clasped her shoulders, he grabbed the sheets the moment she ran her tongue up his hard shaft. He swore an electric current that didn't seem natural shot through him, forcing his back to arch. "Did you do something by any chance?"

She looked up at him, her hair falling over her face. "If you're asking if I gave you a little buzz, I did. Did you like it?" Zulema smiled and more than his cock received a charge.

"Absolutely. I didn't know someone could do that."

"It's a bit of magic I inherited from my warlock father."

"What else can you do?"

"Patience, my prince."

He didn't want to be called a prince since he had done nothing to deserve it, but he'd bring that up later. Zulema continued to lick and suck while she moaned in pleasure. Just as he was about to come, she took hold of his dick and squeezed.

"Enough." He flipped her onto her back and pressed against her wet opening. "I hope you're ready for the ride of your life." So much for having her ride him.

"Show me your magic," she said and then grinned.

ZULEMA WANTED TO appear calm and collected, but that was impossible. Being sassy wasn't her style, but Bevon seemed to bring out her light-hearted side.

He leaned over, cupped her face, and kissed her. She was so distracted by the rampant pulses coursing through her veins that he was halfway inside her before she refocused her attention to this major event in her life. The old Zulema would be questioning what the hell she was doing, but the sexy Fey had her smitten. More than ever, she was convinced they were mates.

Bevon withdrew and slowly eased in again. When he was fully seated, heat swamped her hard, awakening her inner dragon. She drew his face to hers and kissed him like it might be the last time they would be together. It was almost as if he'd put some kind of spell on her!

Zulema expected him to thrust into her again, but instead, he remained in place, and that would not do. She pressed her heals against the mattress and lifted up.

"Someone's eager," Bevon said with too much glee.

"Just move!"

He laughed. "I do adore you."

What happened next transported her to another realm. He kissed, thrust, and plunged again and again, causing every part of her body to explode.

Holy goddess, her dragon exclaimed. *Told you he was our mate.*

You were right.

Bevon dipped his head, dragged his lips down her neck, and kissed her while he hammered into her. With each additional thrust, her climax built until she couldn't take it any longer. Zulema dug her nails into his skin.

"Now!" She wasn't really sure what that meant, but her mind was fogged, and her thoughts had jumbled.

As she dropped her hips and then lifted them again, he tunneled into her and held still. When he slightly bit her shoulder and grunted, her orgasm swooped in. Her mind blanked and her body soared. A second later, he came, his cock pulsing and throbbing, stretching her to the max. Without a doubt, Feys—or maybe it was just Bevon—were larger than any man she'd ever known.

Bevon eventually collapsed and then rolled them over. Zulema lowered her head on his chest as he wrapped his arms around her. For the first time in a long while, she felt safe—a feeling she relished.

HOLDING ZULEMA IN his arms for hours calmed something deep inside of him, but it also built a worry, a worry that escalated the longer that group of Zon were out there. Forcing all but the most pleasant thoughts aside, he eventually managed to catch a few winks.

When sunlight streamed in the window, he eased himself away from his mate. The fact Zulema didn't wake told him she felt safe with him, and that gave him a lot of satisfaction.

With a sweep of a hand, he cleaned up and dressed. Bevon then teleported to the kitchen. While he could use more magic to produce a meal worthy of kings, he wanted to show her that he could be like any other Tarradon man—albeit one who could teleport and protect her better.

He looked around the kitchen, wondering if he could pull this off. Making coffee would be easy. He filled the pot and started the coffee maker, a piece of machinery that didn't exist on Feyrion. Next, he located the skillets that he'd use to cook the food. Lastly, he grabbed the needed ingredients from the refrigerator.

Bevon was halfway through the meal preparation when Zulema

came out of the bedroom dressed adorably in one of his shirts. The fact her nipples pressed through the thin material had his cock turning rigid in no time.

He smiled. "Good morning. How did you sleep?"

She swiped a hand over her eyes. "Good." She moved closer. "You cook?"

"My sisters would say no, but you can be the judge."

"Is today the day?"

He assumed that meant it was the day he would pretend to die. "Yes, but I'd like to visit Tory's cousin, Camden, first to find out whether the medallion has a tracking device in it. The answer might change how we do things."

"That makes sense. Is the coffee ready?" she asked.

"It is."

Zulema fixed herself a cup. "Do you want one?"

"Most definitely."

She poured him a cup and handed it to him. "Why don't you let me fix breakfast?"

Now he was insulted, but he didn't want her first meal to taste bad. "Be my guest. It will give me time to hone our plan."

While Zulema worked her own kind of magic in the kitchen, he drew a map for how he pictured the supposed killing to go down. Once he talked it over with Zulema, he'd share his idea with his sisters.

Less than fifteen minutes later, she placed two plates on the table. "I'm impressed," he said.

"Wait until you taste it."

Zulema picked up her fork and then stopped. "Before we visit this tech genius, I'll need to grab more clothes."

He didn't like that idea of her leaving his house as it would make her more vulnerable. Bevon did a hand sweep and dressed her in jeans and a pretty pink top.

She looked down. "For real? That was great."

That gave him such satisfaction. "Check out the underwear."

Zulema peeked down her shirt. "My bra is bright red. I'm highly impressed."

"Thank you. If the medallion is a tracking device, I'd rather have you stay here, but I know you'll just argue with me."

"You got that right, but can't this cousin disable it so Valoric can't find me?" she asked.

"I imagine he could, but I think we can use it to our advantage."

She smiled. "You mean by leaving it in strategic places to make Valoric believe I'm someplace else?"

He tapped his forehead. "Exactly."

"After Tory's cousin finishes examining the medallion, we'll head back here and leave it, if need be."

She made a valid point. "You got it."

Zulema seemed to work to hold in a smile, as they both dug into their meals. Once they finished, Bevon stood and inhaled deeply. Because time was an issue, Bevon used magic to clean up.

Zulema's eyes widened. "Wow. Can you clean the whole house like that?"

"I can, but I won't. At least not right now. We need to visit Camden to see what he can tell us about the medallion."

Zulema pushed back her chair. "Do I need to take anything?"

"No." Bevon wrapped an arm around her waist and kissed her. "Sorry, I had to have my morning lovin'."

Even after the amazing lovemaking last night, he feared he might be moving too fast. Zulema appeared to be a bit weary at times, but Bevon was confident that he could charm her into falling in love with him. Naturally, he expected the gods of fate to lend a hand.

"I'm not sorry." The grin on her face implied they'd be mates very soon. Guess he was wrong about moving too fast.

"I can't tell you how happy I am to hear that." He tapped her butt. "Let's go."

Bevon would have called Camden to let him know they would be stopping by, but he didn't want to disturb Tory for the phone number. A moment later, they arrived at Tory's cousin's front door.

Bevon knocked, but no one answered.

"Tory said her cousin is often in his basement doing experiments. How about we check?" he suggested.

"Sure."

They teleported to the basement. Sure enough, Camden was bent over some metal structure, wearing his goggles with his music blaring. So as not to surprise him too much, Bevon turned down the volume.

Camden jerked to attention and then slapped a hand over his chest. "This is a surprise," he said.

"Sorry, but we need your help."

Tory's cousin took off his goggles, set them down, and faced them. "Tell me."

Chapter Fourteen

AFTER INTRODUCING ZULEMA to Camden, Bevon did a great job at detailing the current tense situation.

"Let me see this intriguing device," Camden said. "I've never examined a portal opener before."

Zulema handed it to him. "We fear that Derrick has been keeping track of where I am. For all I know, he is watching me now."

Camden nodded. "Give me a few minutes."

"Sure," Bevon said.

She would have suggested that they take a stroll or enjoy the town, but being in public probably wasn't smart. "How about we sit upstairs and plan your death?" she whispered.

"You like saying that don't you?" He winked.

"No! I need you alive." While that was quite true, Zulema enjoyed teasing him.

"Is it because you need me to protect your family?"

Zulema punched him in the arm. "Don't be silly. I do need you for that, but after last night, I can tell you have other uses."

Bevon laughed and then turned back to Camden. "We'll be upstairs."

"This shouldn't take too long. Be up shortly."

Once they were seated, she had to make sure he understood that she'd need her crossbow in order to do the pretend deed.

"Where is it?"

"In my suitcase that is at the hotel. It folds up."

"How about we get it? You can go in, claim your suitcase, while I'll be right next to you—cloaked, of course."

"I like that idea. Since Camden has the medallion, the Zon will think I'm still here, assuming they are tracking me."

"I agree."

Because Camden needed some time to investigate the piece of jewelry, they teleported to the hotel where she had checked out. They were able to return quickly.

"Let's see this instrument of death," he said once they were back at Camden's house.

She pulled it out of her suitcase and assembled it. "I'm thinking we should change the tip to maybe rubber?"

"I like that idea, especially if I wear any kind of protective vest. I don't want the arrow to bounce off it."

"That would be bad, if the Zon are watching."

Before they could outline the plan further, Camden came upstairs. "I have to say I am impressed with the technology of this thing."

"It came from my home world," Bevon said.

"That explains a lot, but yes, there is a tracking device. See this small button here?" He pointed to it.

They both leaned close. "Yes," she said.

"That deactivates the device."

Bevon slipped it out of Camden's hand. "Thank you. We'll have to discuss if it's wise to shut it off or not. And, can we trouble you for something else?"

"Name it."

"Can you replace the metal tip on this arrow with a rubber one?"

Camden studied it. "This is fine workmanship, but sure. You want it to be a suction cup type of device?"

Bevon looked over at Zulema. "That would work."

Camden touched his forefinger to his forehead. "Be right back."

It was only a few minutes before he returned. "What do you think?" He twirled the arrow around.

"Perfect," she said. "One more thing. The person who gave it to me claimed I could contact him with this device. Do you know how?" Zulema had been able to receive Valoric's message, but she didn't know if sending was possible using that same button.

"Yes. I didn't do it, but I believe if you press these two gems simultaneously, it should work."

Only then did she recall something like that in the dossier. "Should I need to contact him, I'll give it a try."

Bevon stood. "Camden, I'm going to put a protection aura around your house to keep out people you don't want here. The Zon might be tracking Zulema to your house as we speak. They would demand to know why Zulema was here."

Camden shrugged. "If needed, I can tell them that she wanted a sleeker arrow, one with a tip laced with treniam."

"You are a genius," she said. "That is smart, especially since I couldn't be sure whether I could get close enough to Bevon to drag the poisonous plant down his arm or not. He could be wearing a long-sleeved shirt. If the arrow tip had been hollowed out and filled with a liquid form of the poison, it would kill him quicker."

Camden smiled. "Exactly. Just make certain you don't really do it."

"Don't worry, I don't have any treniam," she assured him.

Camden faced her. "I hope you and Bevon take down this group. If you need any help, you know the my family is here for you."

She shook his hand. "Much appreciated."

Together, she and Bevon teleported back to his cabin. At this hour she didn't expect to see Fay in his home, but there she was.

"Ah, the bracelets," Bevon said with a lot of excitement.

Zulema looked up at him. "What are they for?"

His sister stepped closer. "Not being able to communicate tele-pathically can be a problem at times. By both of you wearing these, you can." She showed Zulema how it worked.

"Can I try it?" This was amazing. It was almost as if she lived in a different time and place.

"Of course."

Zulema had never been able to telepath with anyone, and her pulse soared at the idea. She placed the stone on the bracelet over her heart. *"Can you hear me, Bevon?"* she asked in her mind, hoping this was how it was done.

"I can." He smiled.

Zulema faced Fay. "That is fantastic. Thank you."

"I want everything to go as planned."

"Me, too."

"Just know that this is a locator bracelet too," he said.

"That gives me some peace knowing if the Zon take me, you'll be able to find me."

"I will."

Once his sister disappeared, Zulema faced Bevon. "Thank you again. Being able to talk to you with my mind is incredible."

"Perhaps you'd like to celebrate. It will be my last day on Tarradon for a while." Bevon cupped her face and kissed her.

Even with all that had happened, a rush of lust filled every cell in her body. Zulema pressed her body against his and deepened the kiss. The logical side of her mind should be questioning this, but the emotional side refused. She wanted Bevon, plain and simple.

He broke the kiss and leaned back. "Then may I?" he asked.

She wasn't sure what he was referring to, but she was game with whatever he wanted to do. Knowing that this house was sheltered from all Zon allowed her to let go and relax.

"Of course." She raised her eyebrows.

He swept a hand down her body and then down his. What happened to her clothes she didn't know, but who was she to question the magic of the Fey?

AFTER THEIR INTENSE and wonderful lovemaking session, Zulema awoke snuggled in Bevon's arms, not wanting this day to end. He looked so cute with his dirty blond hair tangled, and the scruff on his face fuller.

"You okay?" he asked.

"Yes and no. I know we have to do this, but I have a sense something bad is going to happen."

He ran a knuckle down her cheek. "Nothing will happen. I have it under control." He leaned over and kissed her but didn't deepen the kiss like she wanted. "If I get started, I won't be able to stop."

"I get it. How long do you think you'll have to be in hiding on Feyrion?" she asked.

He lifted a shoulder. "Hard to say. I'm not counting on the Zon being reliable with their promise to return your sister and your friend."

Injustice roiled inside of her. "Then I'll save them myself."

Bevon clasped her hand. "Not alone. Ask Kenton, Tory, or anyone in her family to help. But here's the problem. Even if you bring them to the cabin where they will be safe, who is to say Derrick won't capture someone else?"

"I got the sense that he just wants justice for his mate's death."

"I hope you are right. Once the coast is clear, you can go to Feyrion, and together we can find the real killer."

"And then what? Contact Valoric and prance this person in front of him? Who's to say he'll believe that this new person is the real killer? He'll know you're a liar once you've pretended to be dead."

He tapped his head. "I can say I died, but that being immortal, I awoke."

"Seriously? He won't believe it. That will make me an accomplice in this farce."

"Okay, I'll go with my other plan."

"What would that be?" Bevon could be frustrating in his carefree attitude.

"Let's take one step at a time. You pretend to kill me. As I am dying, I will enlist the help of my sisters to take my supposedly dead body back to Feyrion for a proper royal burial."

"It's possible the Zon will contact Kenton and maybe Tory to find out if you really died."

"True. It would look like something is awry if Kenton and his mate don't return home. I'll take care of that, but in the meantime, you will go back to your house after I've died. Your mission will have been accomplished. Once you believe I'm dead, you should leave."

That made sense. "I imagine Derrick will contact me at some point. The only way he'll know if this was a ruse would be if he has someone inside your family to tell him that you are alive and well."

Bevon's eyes widened. "Shit. Didn't you say that Tristan was the one who told Derrick that I killed my cousin?"

"Yes."

He nodded. "I'll have to make sure that Tristan is kept at a distance—at least for a little while."

That was a curious comment. "What are you thinking?"

He tapped her nose. "I have an idea that involves magic." He said the last word with flair.

Since Bevon didn't seem to be all that forthcoming with his plan, she thought it best to get this terrible event out of the way. "Ready?"

"Yes."

They'd discussed the events that would lead up to his *death*, and Zulema thought the plan a sound one. She slipped out of bed and picked up her clothes.

"Would you like a different outfit?" he asked. "That doesn't look like what an assassin would wear."

"That is sweet of you, but I hardly think walking out of the house in camouflage makes sense. We need this to look like an ordinary day."

"You're right."

She donned the clothes she had on this morning—ones he'd created. They were amazingly comfortable. "Do you have to worry about my size when you make these?"

"No. The clothes conform to your body shape."

Zulema didn't think she'd ever get used to those kinds of abilities. They decided that she'd leave her crossbow in his house until she needed it. In theory, Bevon would be so smitten with her that he wouldn't know she had brought it with her in the first place. Farfetched perhaps, but she thought Valoric wouldn't care as long as Bevon died.

Bevon opened his hand to reveal a palmful of green leaves. "This is the closest plant to treniam. I doubt anyone other than a Fey could tell it wasn't the real deal."

She took it from him and placed it in her pocket. Zulema inhaled, ready for probably the biggest assignment of her life.

They wanted the Zon to think that Zulema had seduced him so that she would be close enough to rub the treniam on his arm. Good thing he was wearing a short-sleeved T-shirt, or their plan would be more difficult. Using another bit of magic, he'd disguised the metal chest protector under his shirt.

"Where should we do this?" she asked.

"Let's take a romantic stroll toward the eternal flame. We'll stop, and then you'll do your nasty deed."

Even though this wasn't real, her heart fluttered. Zulema found it hard to believe that the Zon was near to watch the big event, but she couldn't chance they weren't. It wasn't as if she'd told Derrick when the mission would take place. Yes, she was carrying the medallion, hoping it led the Zon to their location, but they wouldn't know the timing.

They walked out the front door, something she didn't recall them doing before. Usually, they teleported. Acting like non-magical humans almost seemed strange.

Once on the path, she squeezed his hand, let go, and pressed the jewel on the bracelet to her heart. *If I don't do this now, I will lose my courage.*

He stopped and turned her to face him. *I'm ready.*

Bevon leaned over and kissed her. While they'd planned this, she sensed he was trying to calm her. Zulema pulled the plant from her pocket and dragged it down his arm. As if a hundred cameras were watching, Bevon moaned, staggered backward, and dropped to the ground.

"You bitch," he called out.

Even though he was acting, his words stung. Pushing aside her feelings, Zulema laughed. "That's for killing your cousin."

"I didn't kill Tamarella."

"That's not what I heard." This whole play acting made her sick.

Because Bevon would be contacting his sisters soon, Zulema teleported back to his cabin, grabbed her rubber-tipped crossbow, and returned to exact the fatal blow. "Just in case you manage to survive, I want to finish this."

Standing a few feet from him, she loaded her bow, aimed for his heart, and shot. Bevon grabbed the arrow and screamed in apparent pain. The packet of red dye between his shirt and breast plate broke as planned. She knelt down, felt for a pulse, and pretended as if she didn't find one. "Good riddance, Fey."

They expected someone might check out her claim that he was dead, so Zulema planned to stay around for another minute. Because his sisters would be showing up shortly, she teleported behind a tree to keep watch. Once they came, Zulema would head back to her house and await Derrick Valoric's response. If his two sisters remained away, Zulema would do a pretend second check on the body and then leave.

Just when Zulema was about to do her last check, a man wearing a hoodie emerged from the woods with a crossbow in his hand. What the hell? He rushed over to Bevon, looked around probably to make sure no one would come to Bevon's rescue, and then kicked him hard enough to roll him onto his stomach. Every cell in Zulema's body shot to high alert. She raised her bow, unsure of whether to kill this man. Her only hesitation was that the Zon might be watching her. If they expected this new assassin to contact headquarters, and he didn't, more of her friends and family might be in jeopardy.

Bevon was immortal she reminded herself, even though he was now face down, not making a sound or moving.

Zulema touched the communication bracelet to her chest. *"The man plans to kill you. What should I do?"* she telepathed.

"Nothing. Go now," came his response.

Hearing his voice in her head sent a trickle of relief through her. With Bevon lying motionless, the second assassin lifted his bow and shot Bevon in the back where his metal plate did not cover him. The surprise and pain must have been intense, yet he made no sound. Why hadn't he teleported out of there? Or better yet, why hadn't his sisters or brother come to his rescue? Stubborn man.

As much as Zulema wanted to see what would happen next, it was best if she left.

Chapter Fifteen

B EVON CLAMPED DOWN on his jaw in order to endure the pain without making a sound. Slowing his heart rate to appear dead was not an easy task, but he forced his body to calm. While he might not die from the wound—unless the arrow tip was covered in treniam—the pain was nonetheless intense.

"Where are you, sisters?"

"We're coming."

Footsteps of someone running away sounded. The next thing he knew, Bevon was on his bed in the cabin instead of on Feyrion like he was supposed to be.

"Hold still," Fay said.

She pulled out the arrow from his back, and the strong ache caused him to black out. When he roused, both of his sisters were holding hands and sitting at the foot of his bed.

"How do you feel?" Meena asked.

"Like I was shot with an arrow. Who the hell was that guy?" he asked.

"You tell us," Fay said. "We waited for you to give the all clear before we came out. By the time you called us, someone had shot you. We found Zulema's harmless arrow broken off underneath you, but someone else had been there."

"It wasn't Zulema. She did what she was supposed to do. She saw him and warned me."

"We need to speak with her then," Fay said.

"The blood packet you placed on your chest made the injury look very real. I'm surprised the person thought the need to kill a dead person," Meena added.

"I was wondering the same thing. And how did Valoric know when the attack would take place?" There was no way Zulema had colluded with that man. She was Bevon's mate!

He tried to sit up, but Fay pressed on his shoulder. "Rest."

He waved her off. "I'll heal. Where is Zulema?"

"I'm guessing she is at home. Wasn't that the plan?"

"Yes." He tapped his bracelet. *"Zulema,"* he telepathed. *"Even though you saw that person shoot me in the back, I'm okay. Can you leave the medallion at your house and come to the cabin now?"* He didn't need that vindictive ass to follow her here. *"I need to know what you saw."* It took all of his strength to ask that much.

When she didn't answer, worry crept into his soul. Valoric wouldn't have punished her for fulfilling her mission unless he believed she'd faked it. Assuming the second assassin was sent by Valoric as insurance, he could never know if Zulema's first arrow killed him or not.

Footsteps sounded as Zulema ran into the bedroom, and a calm shot through his veins. She sat on the edge of the bed and placed a hand on his arm. "Are you okay?"

"I'll be fine."

"I wanted to kill the man who shot you. I wished you hadn't insisted that I leave."

"He could have killed you next. I'm betting this guy was there to make sure that I died, though how Valoric knew today was the day, I don't know."

Her pretty little mouth pinched. "Neither do I, but how dare Derrick think I didn't have the guts to kill you."

Bevon appreciated her attitude. "Right now, we have more important things to worry about."

"Like having a funeral in Feyrion?"

"Yes," he said. "But first, tell me what you saw."

Zulema explained about the man with the hood. "I couldn't see his face."

"How tall was he?"

She hesitated. "That's hard to say. He was hunched over you, but if I had to guess, I'd say a few inches taller than you."

Bevon sucked in a breath, sending a sharp pain to his back. Damn it. "That doesn't eliminate Derrick as the assassin, but I imagine he'd send one of the Zon to do his dirty work."

"I agree. Derrick seems too arrogant to get his hands dirty, but why not send this man in the first place? If he didn't trust me to do the job, why bother with me?"

"That is a good question. Maybe he figured you'd be able to find the treniam. It is almost impossible to kill me without it. Only if he saw you rub it on my arm would he send in the second attacker to insure I was truly dead." He worked at a smile. "You know us pesky Fey. We're tough to kill."

"That's a good thing." Zulema looked up at his sisters and shook her head. "I'm sorry. I should have anticipated Valoric's move, that he'd want to ensure Bevon had died."

He clasped her hand. "You couldn't have known. But don't worry, I'll be good as new soon."

Her smile came out weak. "I know. What now?"

"As much as I'd like you with me, you need to return home. If Derrick contacts you, let me know right away using the bracelet."

Zulema let out a long sigh. "I will."

His mate was fiercely independent. "Promise me one thing."

"What?"

"Do not try to save your sister and your friend by yourself—or at all for that matter."

Not that she knew where they were. Zulema glanced downward at her hands. "Now that you're dead, why not? I can teleport in and save them."

"I know, but who's to say Valoric won't retaliate? We want him to think you trust him. You completed your assignment and believe he'll return your sister and friend. Give him a chance to do so."

"Maybe you're right. What will you be doing?" she asked.

"Recuperating while my family tells everyone I died. Don't worry, I have a plan."

She gritted her teeth at him. "There you go with your plans again. Are you going to let me in on this one?"

"Soon. Now go." He wanted to kiss her, but then he'd desire her even more, and right now, he wasn't fit enough for that.

ZULEMA TELEPORTED HOME, happy she'd seen for herself that Bevon was okay. She paced her living room, trying to figure out why Derrick had sent a second assassin. It might not matter. As long as Derrick believed Bevon was dead, he'd return her friend and sister and leave her alone. Or was she being naïve?

She fixed herself a sandwich, but it didn't satisfy her in the least. Being left out of the loop was totally frustrating. The problem was that she had no idea when Bevon would tell her she was free to visit him on Feyrion. While she could go on her own, using the medallion would be stupid. Derrick could follow her—or hire someone to.

Had this been a real mission, what would she do next? That was easy. She'd look for another job. Ugh. Being a bodyguard required vigilance, and right now, she'd be looking over her shoulder for someone to take her down, instead of worrying about who might want to harm the person she was paid to protect.

Often, she would take a few days off between jobs to mentally regroup. That might be her best move now. While returning to Edendale would be a pleasant diversion, it might signal to Derrick that she had connected with Bevon after his death.

"Damn you, Derrick Valoric."

Aislin, her friend, had uncovered a few things about the man. Since Zulema needed to do something until Bevon gave her the all clear, she located the information her friend had sent her to see if there was anything that could be done to bring down this man— from a distance of course.

For the next few hours, she studied the file and was even able to add some information of her own. She had to hand it to Valoric and his employers. They'd covered their tracks well. When her research was done, Zulema considered taking some time to explore parts of Tarradon she'd never had the chance to see before. Since she'd have no need of the medallion, Derrick wouldn't expect her to carry it with her. Despite that, she had the sense the Zon might use other methods to keep track of her.

The problem was that sightseeing didn't appeal to her at the moment. Her only choice was to find Derrick. Then she'd demand he return her sister and friend. She could only hope he wouldn't require her to do more of his bidding. If he did that, she'd have to kill him.

THREE DAYS!! ZULEMA wasn't sure who she was angrier with— Bevon or Derrick Valoric. Her sister and Aislin should have been freed by now. Even though she'd followed the instructions both Camden and Derrick had given her regarding contacting Valoric, he never responded. Asshole.

As for Bevon? Her bracelet didn't seem to be working either. She assumed that he would communicate with her telepathically at some point to let her know it was okay to go to Feyrion. But apparently, she was wrong. She tried to initiate the contact, but he must have turned off the device, though she had no idea how or why.

Considering his family was in charge of the portal, one of them should return at some point to guard it. She'd hoped one of his family members would contact her to let her know what was going on, but they never did. It was possible the funeral took longer than on Tarradon, since it might involve more preparation. After all, Bevon was a prince. Not that it mattered in the big scheme, but were invitations sent, or did the royal family telepath the details to everyone?

The more time she spent thinking about his family, the more questions she had.

If Bevon had contacted her, he'd tell her to wait it out, but standing around was terribly frustrating. Zulema was a warrior, and as such, had to do something. Using the medallion to get into Feyrion would be risky, but maybe she should chance it. Just as she picked up the device, Fay appeared.

"Zulema, what are you doing?"

Shit. Caught. Did they have cameras in her house to watch her? That would be creepier than the Zon. "Checking to see if Derrick sent a message. He hasn't, and I'm losing my patience."

"We'll deal with him shortly."

"Is Bevon okay? It's been days."

She smiled. "Yes. He's good as new. Now that the funeral is over, he'd like you to come to Feyrion."

Her pulse soared. "Finally!"

"Not that Bevon can't supply you with what you need, but you might feel better if you packed a few things."

"Thank you. Give me a sec."

"While you do that, I will check on your sister and your friend."

Zulema wanted to say she'd like to tag along, but she had the sense Fay would not allow that. "Thank you."

Fay disappeared, and Zulema rushed to pack. Knowing that Bevon could provide most of what she needed, she only tossed in a few essentials. When she returned to the living room, Fay was there.

Zulema rushed up to her. "How are they?"

"They are both in a rather nice room with a guard standing watch. I tried to find out the agenda, but I didn't see anything to indicate when they might be released."

Zulema touched Fay's arm. "Thank you. That helps a lot knowing they aren't being tortured."

She nodded. "Ready to return to Feyrion?"

"I am."

"Maybe you should put the medallion in a more secure spot than on top of your desk."

Zulema wasn't sure why. "Do you think the Zon will try to steal it while I'm gone?" She had assumed Derrick had two medallions, but maybe this was the only one.

Fay shrugged. "Anything is possible."

The perfect place would be in a box that she kept in the back of her closet. It would take someone weeks to unearth it. She teleported to her room, stashed it securely, and returned. "Let's go."

Fay hooked arms with her and teleported them to the forest where they went through a portal to Feyrion. Zulema expected to be escorted to the main castle. Instead, they arrived in front of a rather modest home at the edge of a large pond surrounded by trees. "What are we doing here?" Zulema asked.

"Bevon is here. We don't want him running around the castle when he is supposed to be dead."

Zulema clamped a hand over her mouth. "The servants don't know the truth?" She hadn't thought of that.

"Not yet. When this is all over, we will reveal everything to them."

It was still terrible. Even though Bevon didn't visit Feyrion often, he was their prince, and as such, would be revered. "I see."

"Come on."

They walked the last few feet to the door instead of teleporting inside. Fay knocked, which Zulema found to be odd. Zulema shifted on her feet, anxiously needing to see a healthy Bevon.

A man about the same height as Bevon, with short, dark brown hair answered. He was wearing black glasses and had on a rather strange outfit that looked like harem pants and a matching shirt.

"Well, what do you think?" the man asked.

"Ah, think about what?"

"My new look."

Zulema had no idea who this man was. She looked over at Fay, but she was gone. What was up with that? Well, crap. "I'm looking for Bevon."

He laughed, and the sound altered something inside her, which was impossible. "You've found him, princess."

Chapter Sixteen

ZULEMA DIDN'T UNDERSTAND. No one called her princess but Bevon, and she didn't like it one bit that this man thought he could. "What have you done with him?"

The man smiled and opened his arms. "I'm right here."

She looked behind this annoying person. "I don't see him."

He lowered his arms. "I see you'll need some convincing. Please come in. While this isn't as nice as the castle, it's a bit better than my cabin in the woods—not that I'm complaining."

He led her over to a sofa that faced a large picture window overlooking a lake. The view was spectacular. "It's really pretty here," she said a bit begrudgingly.

"I'm glad you like it. I have a feeling we'll be here a while."

She wasn't staying with him if that is what he thought. "Why is that?"

"Because we have to find who killed Tamarella."

"We?"

He blew out a breath. "I need to explain what happened after my supposed death."

This stranger acted as if he was Bevon, but how could that be? "I'm confused."

Two beers magically appeared in his hands, and he handed her one. "Let me start from the beginning. I am Bevon, only I look different. That was my grand plan."

"Did you have plastic surgery or something?" It wasn't possible to change a person in three days.

"No. As you have seen first-hand, my mother is very powerful."

He held up a hand. "And yes, we'll sneak a quick visit with your mother in a bit. She is recovering quite well."

Zulema's pulse shot up just hearing her mother was improving. It was something she never imagined would ever happen. "Thank you."

No one but Bevon could have known all of this. Maybe he was Bevon. "Please continue with your story."

"It's hardly a story. We wanted the staff to believe I had died. A closed casket was necessary because my face was severely marred—or so the story went."

It was a bit comforting to know that funerals on Feyrion were similar to those on Tarradon—or at the least the idea that they used caskets. "Then what?"

"My mother put a spell on me that changed my appearance. I assure you no scalpel was used in the process. As this new man, I plan to claim we came here to investigate Tamarella's death."

She sucked in a breath. "I like that idea." Assuming he was really Bevon, and this wasn't some trick. "I could still be Anna DeLeon, and I've returned with an investigator."

His eyes widened. "I like it. Who shall I be?"

"Someone from Tarradon, I suspect."

He smiled. "I'll tell everyone that I'm Derrick Valoric."

She laughed. "That could work unless he's visited here before, and people recognize him."

"Oh, but he has. It's how my mother knew how to change my face, so that I now look like him."

Zulema scooted away from him. "You look like Derrick? Why him?"

"Asking questions about who killed his fated mate makes sense. People, especially Tristan, won't question it."

"It's still wrong. Can you have her change you back again?"

"What? Don't you find me handsome?" Bevon grinned.

"No!"

He scooted over, pulled Zulema close and kissed her. While

waves of pleasure shot through her, when she opened her eyes, her lust diminished. Zulema pushed him away. "I can't."

Bevon groaned. "I understand. I was worried this might happen. You're infatuated with my looks. I knew it." He raised his eyes and sighed.

Now that was typical Bevon, and Zulema couldn't help but punch him. "I do find the old Bevon good looking, but I'm not shallow."

"Tell me more."

"And feed your ego? Ah…no."

He snapped his fingers. "All right then. I have a suggestion."

She wasn't sure she was going to like this any better than him changing his face to fool everyone. While Zulema now understood the need, she was finding it very hard to even kiss him. "What is it?"

"Do you remember the bartender at Wings?"

"Yes, but what does that have to do with anything?" Did his mother alter his brain along with his face?

"Hear me out. His name is Finn, and he's mated to Tory's twin sister."

So that was why he was so chatty with the man. It made sense now. "I didn't know."

"You wouldn't. Anyway, he used to live on Earth when he had dreams of a beautiful woman."

She had no idea what any of this had to do with their current situation. "A lot of people have dreams."

He held up a hand. "But his dreams were real, as in Tory's twin sister, Kaleena, was able to dream walk with him. When she was captured by the Royals in Avonbelle, she needed Finn's help."

"From Earth?"

"That was the tricky part." He explained how he was shown a portal and then introduced to the Four Sisters of Fate. "They are four very powerful women—kind of like my mother. Since Finn needed to sneak into the castle undercover, they temporarily created a fake face for him."

"Like your mother did for you."

"Yes. I think they can help us now."

"Even if they can, why not just ask you mother to do it? Not that I mind the trip to Tarradon."

He shrugged. "I've been looking for an excuse to meet these special ladies."

She had no objections. "Are you going to ask them to change you back?" she asked.

"No, but it will be almost as good. I'd tell you the details, but I don't want to get your hopes up."

She was highly skeptical, but this man did act like Bevon, even if he looked different. And Fay would never mislead her. "Why would they help?"

"They know Tory and her family." Bevon ran a hand down Zulema's arm. "I'll ask her to come with us and make the introductions."

Being a witch, Zulema was all for using magic when needed. She just wished she had the ability to help. "I'm game."

He lowered his chin and shifted his gaze to the side. When he nodded, she figured he was communicating with either his mother or his sisters. Possibly, he was talking to his brother and his mate on Tarradon.

Bevon stood and held out his hand. "Ready?"

"What if the Zon are watching, and they see me with Derrick Valoric?" she asked as she placed her hand in his.

He smiled. "You are working for him. I don't think they will question it, unless they talk to him directly. But don't worry, I asked Tory to meet me at their pottery shop. We'll go there, ask for some help, and return. As long as you left the medallion at your house, you should be safe."

She had to trust him. "I did."

They stepped outside where he created a portal. When they stepped through to Tarradon, they ended up in front of a pottery shop—just like he said. Before they took another step, a tall, beautiful blonde woman appeared and turned to face them.

Tory smiled. "Nice to see you again, Zulema. As much as we need to catch up, we need to do something about Bevon's awful face."

Zulema huffed out a laugh. "You don't like it either?"

"No. He told me he looks like the man who kidnapped you. That would give me the creeps."

She didn't want to mislead anyone. "I never saw Derrick's face, but I prefer the original version of Bevon better."

He grinned. Of course. "Shall we, ladies?"

The inside of the store was a total delight. The store was filled with plates, mugs, vases, and a wide assortment of artwork. Tory said everything was produced on site by four very talented women. Two were manning the store. One of the women, the one with almost white hair, came over.

"Tory, this is a nice surprise."

Tory faced her and Bevon. "Poppy, this is my mate's brother, and this is his…ah, friend from another part of Avonbelle."

The slight hesitation implied Tory was going to say mate. While Zulema believed it true, she and Bevon needed to have that conversation soon. They all shook hands.

"What can I do for you?" Poppy asked.

"May we speak in private?" Bevon asked.

While only one other shopper was in the store, Zulema was glad he didn't want to chance that somehow the woman was a member of the Zon. Farfetched for sure but still possible.

"Of course." She led them to a room that contained a four-seater table as well as a kiln along with rows and rows of unglazed pottery. Once they were seated, Poppy asked what they needed.

Bevon gave a brief rundown of how he came to have his face change. "The problem is that Zulema can't get over the fact that I look like her abductor."

Poppy's eyes widened. "I can see why. What would you like me to do?"

"Can you put a spell on me—or maybe it will be on Zulema—that allows her to see the real me? As soon as the ass who is responsible for all the trouble has been taken care of, I'll have my mother change me back."

"She's the queen of Feyrion, is she not?"

"She is."

Poppy pushed back her chair. "Let me get my sister, Magnolia. Together, we should be able to solve your problem."

She disappeared and returned a second later. "This is Magnolia."

Wow. The two couldn't be more different. Magnolia had wavy black hair. "Thank you for helping me," Zulema said.

"Of course."

The two sisters held hands and closed their eyes. Their lips moved slightly, but Zulema was a bit surprised there was no hand waving, candles suddenly lighting, or herbs magically appearing on the table. When they stopped, Zulema looked over at Bevon and sucked in a breath. "It's you!"

"Thank goddess," he said.

She turned to the special ladies. "I can't thank you enough."

Poppy smiled. "Seeing you two happy is my thanks."

That might have been a dumb thing to say, but seeing his face again tongue-tied her.

Bevon grinned. "Does that mean I can have a kiss?"

Heat raced up her face, mostly because three people were watching. "A quick one."

Zulema leaned over and kissed him briefly, despite her body demanding more.

"Later then?" he asked, as if he could read her mind.

"For sure."

He stood and Zulema followed. Once outside the store, Bevon hugged Tory. She in turn hugged Zulema. "Welcome to the family," Tory said.

That sensation of belonging provided much needed warmth and comfort. "Thank you."

"My pleasure."

Tory teleported, probably to her home. Most likely because Bevon didn't want anyone to see him create a portal, he teleported them to some high mountain crest where the view took her breath away. The landscape wasn't as bright or as green as the mountains on Feyrion, but this site was equally as impressive.

"Alone at last," he said with that devilish look in his eye that she'd come to enjoy.

Zulema wagged a finger at him. "Don't get any ideas."

He laughed. "About what? I was merely mentioning it, because I can now create a portal, and no one will see us. You weren't referring to having hot, desperate sex with me, were you?"

She couldn't stop the heat from racing up her body. "Never."

"I can tell when you're lying, princess."

"Okay, maybe I was thinking about some carnal pleasure. It's been days since I've seen you. All that worry had built up a small desire."

"Only a small desire? You can't fool me."

The man was so infuriating. "Fine. A huge desire. What do you have in mind?"

One moment they were on top of this isolated mountain top fully clothed, and the next she was naked.

"Bevon!"

"What? You aren't shy, are you?"

"Why don't you kiss me and find out?"

Chapter Seventeen

WAVES OF NEED in epic proportions swelled inside Bevon. Staying away from his mate for so many days had ratcheted up his desire something fierce. Not wanting this experience to be uncomfortable in any way, he swept a hand to create a blanket.

"Shall we?" he asked.

"Let me divest you of your clothes first." Zulema wagged a finger. "And no help from the magical realm, okay?"

He couldn't help but grin. To see his mate so forward, thrilled him. "I promise."

"Take off your shoes," she commanded.

"I thought you were going to remove my clothes." Bevon wasn't sure why he enjoyed challenging her so much. Zulema planted a hand on her hip. "Okay, okay. Shoes off."

She watched as he shucked them. "Good. Now hold still."

Zulema stepped behind him, slid her hands under his shirt, and slowly lifted the material. When the shirt was almost to his shoulders, she placed her cheek against his back and inhaled.

He chuckled. "What are you doing?"

"Memorizing your scent in case you decide you need another new face, and I can't see the old one."

Never had a woman ever said anything so romantic to him before. "Would you like a key phrase that you can ask me, so you'll know it's me for sure?"

She let go of the material and stepped to the front. "I like that idea. What do you have in mind?" she asked as she took off his shirt. Her eyes widened. "Whoa. Daylight shows off your body wonderfully."

"That's not a real phrase," he said, teasing her.

"Sorry. You distracted me."

Bevon held in a smile. "Seriously, you'll know it's me, because I call you princess."

"And if you don't realize your real face isn't appearing to me?"

"Ah…how about when you ask what my pet name for you is, I will say *kill me now?*"

She laughed. "That's not a name, not in the least, but it will do. No one else will think of it."

"Now that our code phrase has been decided upon, prepare to be impressed." Bevon grabbed his woman around the waist, pulled her close, and kissed her. When Zulema melted against him, he couldn't help but use his magic to remove his pants.

She stepped back. "You said you wouldn't use magic."

If she'd sounded the least bit upset, he would have replaced the clothes. "That kiss blocked out all memory of what I promised. Sorry."

Moving closer, Zulema planted her hands on his naked chest, and her fingers burned into his skin. "What's the key phrase you'll use to prove it's you?"

"Kill me now."

She laughed. "Your memory seems fine to me."

"You are too sassy for your own good."

As Bevon kissed her again, he dragged Zulema down to the blanket and pulled her on top of him. Without prompting, she broke the kiss, straddled him, leaned over, and fed him a breast. Excitement and lust soared through him. Zulema was an amazing woman.

He lifted his head to better feast on her. He licked, sucked, and then ran his hands down her back and butt. If she hadn't sat on his cock and then wiggled, he would have been completely absorbed in her offered feast.

A dragon shifter flew high overhead. Damn. Trying to be as unobtrusive as possible, Bevon created an invisibility bubble around them to prevent them from being detected. Safe and sound in their cocoon, he returned to pleasuring her body.

"My turn," she announced.

Before he could object, Zulema slid down and rubbed her face against his cock. The sensation was soft yet sensual—until she grabbed the base and licked the tip. Because he'd been without his mate for days, each touch was like putting a match to a pile of dried leaves. His body caught fire. While Zulema seemed to enjoy licking and sucking his cock until he exploded, he wanted to provide her with some joy of her own. "Enough."

"You're that much of a lightweight?" she asked.

"You are asking for trouble, princess." He flipped them over.

"You know I wasn't finished."

"Uh huh." Bevon kissed her once more. From the way she invited him in, she wasn't upset. Good. Like the warrior that she was, Zulema met his thrusts with conviction, and her intermittent moans added to the enjoyment.

A dragon shifter squawked overhead, and she looked up. "We need to move. It could be the Zon."

The fear in her voice broke the sensual bond. "He can't see us. I put an invisibility shield around us."

Zulema glanced up again. "Are you sure?"

"Have I ever lied? Don't answer that." Even though he didn't think he had. "We're safe."

She returned her focus to him and smiled. "Where were we?"

"That's my girl."

He rolled onto his side and dragged her against him so that almost every part of their bodies was touching.

Zulema smiled. "I like this. Maybe we can just stay here."

He pretended to look crestfallen. "You don't want to catch my cousin's killer and free your family?"

She pinched his shoulder. "Way to bring reality into this."

He was a cad. "How can I make it up to you?"

"Mmm. I'm sure the great lover, Bevon Forrester, can figure it out."

"Great lover, you say?"

She rolled her eyes. "That's what the dossier on you said. The actual words were that you were a womanizer."

"That hurts. Let's see if I can change your perception of me."

She slapped his butt. "Bring it on, Prince Charming."

He laughed and then returned his attention to her divine lips. As much as he, too, wanted to spend a leisurely day making love, they couldn't afford the luxury.

Who was he kidding? Much more of this touching would cause him to explode before he wanted to anyway. Lasting all day with Zulema truly was impossible.

Bevon flipped her over and then slid between her legs. He bent her knees and then ran his tongue over her wet opening.

"Yes!" she moaned. "You are a true master."

"Only with you, my love."

She dug her rather sharp nails into his shoulders and wiggled her hips. Her eyes had turned the prettiest shade of purple, and her skin had heated. Bevon dragged his hands up to her breasts, cupped one, and lightly pinched the nipple of the other. Zulema lifted her hips.

"Take me," she panted.

He loved her desperate tone. Truth be told, he needed her more than she needed him.

Bevon sat up, drew her onto her elbows and knees and pressed his dick to her wet opening. The scent of her sex and the delightful aroma of her skin drove him crazy. Using all of his control, he eased into her. She bucked at first and then widened her legs to accommodate him.

Zulema lowered her head to her hands and pressed her hips back. That was about as much as he could handle of this siren. Bevon took hold of her and drove into her over and over again, the white glow around his body growing. Glorious desire and, dare he say, love, flowed through him. It was an emotion he'd never really experienced quite this way before, but it was overwhelmingly wonderful.

Releasing his hands, Bevon dragged his palms up to her breasts and massaged them. Every time he plucked her nipples, his excitement grew—if that was even possible.

When Zulema arched her back, he tunneled into her one more time, and she clamped down on his cock so hard, he came—and so did she.

Not only did his arms glow, his whole body lit up their intimate bubble. When his dick finishing pulsating, he slid out, rolled onto his back, and drew her on top of him. "I think we should always make love outside."

Her whole body lay limp. "Uh huh."

Bevon held her until the heat from her skin slowly dissipated. After a long rest, he rolled her off of him and magically cleaned them both up before redressing them. "As much as I hate to suggest it, we need to return to Feyrion. We don't want your sister and friend to remain incarcerated any longer than necessary."

She nodded. "Maybe I should try to call Derrick again and demand he send them back."

"Again?"

"He didn't answer the first time. Between my fake arrow and the other assassin's real one, Derrick should be convinced you died. No matter where they look, they won't find you."

He loved her feisty attitude. "If you use the medallion to contact him, what's to say he won't teleport to you and then kidnap you again?"

"Why would he do that?"

"He might have other uses for you."

She let out a long breath. "I was worried about that. By me contacting him, I would, in essence, be giving him my location." Her shoulders drooped. "This sucks. I'm not even sure if we find the killer that he'll stop."

"Then we'll just have to kill him."

She laughed. "Seriously?"

Did she doubt him? "Why not? If he returns your family, I'll reconsider."

Zulema pressed her lips together, and then nodded." Sounds good. Once we find the killer, I will demand an audience with him."

His mate was something else. Bevon made a portal, and they immediately arrived at the cabin where he had been staying. It had been nice to get out, and it had been genius on his part to have a spell that allowed Zulema to see the real him. The last thing he wanted was for her to make love to a man who looked so different.

"Hungry?" he asked.

"Do you eat all the time?"

He planted a hand on his chest. "I need my fuel. In this case, I was thinking of you."

"Fine. I could use a steak, some sautéed vegetables, and maybe a salad."

She was testing him, but that was okay. "Have a seat at the table. We'll need a plan for how to uncover the killer."

Zulema sat. "How about some paper? I like to jot down my ideas."

Paper and a pen appeared before her. A second later, a full meal showed up in front of her. She looked up at him. "You did it!"

"I am a Fey."

"I love that you are."

A part of him had worried that she wouldn't want to be with someone who was so different from herself. Apparently, he'd worried for nothing.

"Eat first and then brainstorm?" she asked.

"Works for me."

Chapter Eighteen

ZULEMA LEANED BACK in her seat. "That might have been the best meal I have ever had. What kind of meat was that?"

"Nothing you would have heard of."

Perhaps it was better if she didn't know. "Regardless, thank you."

"You're welcome." He swept his hand, and the dishes disappeared.

"Whoa." Sure, he'd told her he could clean up using magic, but to witness it was something else altogether.

He grinned. "You'll get used to it. Now, on to why we are here. How do you want to start?"

He was asking her? "How about we speak with Tristan first? Derrick said he claimed you were the killer. He must have based it on some incriminating evidence."

"I wonder why he picked me to point the finger at. I hardly know Tristan. What would be his motive for claiming I killed my own cousin?"

She'd given it some thought. "Maybe it was because you weren't on Feyrion to deny the claim."

"Could be, but I wasn't here when she died either."

"Is Tristan always aware of your comings and goings?" she asked.

"No, but if he'd asked anyone in my family, they would have set him straight."

His family seemed very protective of all of its members. They probably wouldn't have pointed a finger at one of their own, regardless of guilt. "Perhaps Tristan killed Tamarella and had to tell

Derrick something."

Bevon pointed a finger at her. "That begs the question: How did Derrick learn I was the supposed murderer? Did he show up at Tristan's house demanding answers? Or did Tristan go to Tarradon? Though why would he?"

"Good question. Unless Tristan commissioned Derrick to kill you."

"Anything's possible, but I don't see it. If anyone learned of his deceit, he'd die a terrible death."

"Okay. Tristan didn't want you killed. If his family was in dire straights financially, he'd be the last person to want your cousin dead, right?"

"Right."

"Your death wouldn't help him in any way. According to your aunt, both parties saw it as their obligation to help strengthen each family."

He nodded. "There has to be a reason for why Tamarella was killed though, and it might not have anything to do with money."

She snapped her fingers. "Is it possible Derrick planned to kidnap her at the last minute, and Tristan decided that if he couldn't have her, no one could?"

Bevon drummed his fingers on the table. "Excellent point. I could look at the logs to see if he entered the portal, but if Derrick had a special device like he gave to you, he would have avoided me on the Tarradon end and our portal guards on this end."

"We have Derrick, Tristan, and even you. You didn't do it, and I'm thinking Derrick didn't either."

"Why?" he asked.

"I don't see him as the killer even if he could teleport into her room without notice. I also don't see him taking orders from someone on Feyrion."

"Maybe not. The only reason Derrick would have for killing Tam would be if he was convinced his mate planned to go through with the union with Tristan. We could use the same argument. If he couldn't have her, no one could."

"Then why take me? To take the heat off of anyone coming after him for the murder?"

Bevon shook his head. "I don't think so. Just by being on Tarradon, Derrick's fairly safe. Not that we wouldn't go to another realm to find a killer, but we would look here first. I agree, take Derrick off the table."

She scratched off his name. "Next?"

"I suppose Tristan's brother, Carmen, is a suspect."

"Why him? Was he against the union?"

"I'll ask Tally to be sure, but Carmen was always hot headed. He was jealous of his brother."

"Why?"

"Tristan was better looking, smarter, and a more powerful warlock. Perhaps Carmen believed if Tristan spent his time with Tamarella that he would be forgotten."

That was a stretch. "We'll keep him for now. Who else?"

"I could make up something, but without more information, we will be wasting our time."

As if she didn't know that. "Your aunt is still in mourning over her daughter's death. I'm not sure she'll be of much help."

"I might be able to get her to open up."

Zulema couldn't wrap her mind around this. "There has to be a motive for why your cousin was killed. Wounded heart aside, who would benefit the most by her death?"

"I wish I knew." Bevon pushed back his chair, swept his hand, and created a standing white board. "I like to be organized."

Zulema crossed her arms. "Seriously? I thought you took everything in stride."

His face turned a pretty shade of pink.

"Fine. I thought you would like to have a place to write down your thoughts—other than on paper. This way, we can both see it. Just use your finger to draw."

Zulema got up from the table and stepped over to the stand.

"Let's start with Tamarella's family to see if any of them would benefit." She listed their names. "This is an awesome tool."

"I'm glad you like it, but her family would not benefit in the least. They would want the union, because it would make their influence in the realm stronger. While no one spoke of such things, I had the sense Aunt Drina was a little jealous of my mom, because she had most of the power. I think that was why she was willing to go along with the union between Tamarella and Tristan."

"Makes sense. So, no one in your family would have done it?" Wanting to be thorough, she listed Bevon's family next to his aunt's family and then studied the names.

"No. They would have nothing to gain by my cousin's death."

"Okay. Then what about Tristan's family?" she asked.

"Besides, Tristan, there is only his brother Carmen and his parents. It was actually their idea to match Tristan with Tamarella."

"They did seem to benefit the most from the union. You said Tristan's family are warlocks and witches, right?"

"Yes."

"I imagine they would have no problem with Tristan mating with a Fairy?"

"I'm thinking not. Tamarella was a mix between a Fairy and a Fey, but her predominant characteristic was that of a Fey."

This was frustrating. "Someone killed her."

"You've already spoken with Betina, right?"

"I did. Tamarella's handmaiden either didn't know anything or she was lying. I just couldn't tell which."

"This might be harder than I thought. Someone has to know something. I say we go to my aunt's house. I'll pretend to be Derrick who has just arrived from Tarradon."

"Why would your aunt let Derrick in? Unless you tell her the truth that it is really you."

He shook his head. "I can't trust that one of the staff isn't in cahoots with the killer."

Damn. "Who will you question? Your aunt or your uncle? Or

are you thinking Betina might still be there?"

"I don't know. I don't see Betina as the killer. I imagine her job was rather nice. Losing it would cause her financial hardship."

"I'm sure it would," Zulema said. "Then how about we head to town and ask around? When I first arrived, I went to a coffee shop. The girl behind the counter was very forthcoming with information. If Feyrion is anything like where I live, the death of a royal will be the main topic of conversation for weeks."

He smiled. "That is an excellent idea."

Bevon grabbed her hand, and they teleported to the middle of town. Zulema enjoyed the fact that they could flit from one place to another without causing a stir in this realm. "The coffee shop I went to is over there," she said.

"I've been there—or rather Bevon has. I could use a good cup of coffee."

"Remember, you aren't from here," she said.

Bevon tapped his temple. "I got this."

She was glad someone did. When she spotted the chatty counter girl she'd first met, Zulema relaxed. Because the café was abuzz with noise, no one would be able to hear them—unless Feys had super hearing. "That's her."

He inhaled. "I just have to remember I'm Derrick Valoric from Tarradon."

Frequently, Zulema had to call the people she was guarding by a different name. This would be no different. When she walked up to the counter, the girl looked up and smiled. "You're the one from Tarradon. Did you ever find the Warnom house?"

Zulema smiled. "I did and thank you. I was saddened to learn that my friend, Tamarella Warnom, had been murdered though. I had no idea she had died, or I wouldn't have come." Zulema thought that tidbit would make for better conversation.

"I didn't know you were a friend of the family." Her brows rose. "You said the princess was murdered? I thought it was suicide."

She looked over at Bevon. "That's why I'm here. I'm a private investigator from Tarradon," he said.

"Oh."

While Zulema wanted to question this girl further, it would be friendlier if they ordered first then picked her brain. "Could I have a coffee? Black, please."

"Sure, and for you, sir?" Her demeanor turned professional.

He looked over the mounted menu. "A number seven. Oh, and two sweet rolls."

Clearly, this man didn't have to worry about his weight. Zulema wouldn't be surprised if he swept a hand down his body to sculpt it. No diet or exercise needed.

"I'll bring it over to you. Have a seat."

They grabbed a booth near the door. "You want to ask your questions first?" she asked. "You are the private investigator." Zulema thought that role fit him well.

"Since she knows you, you start," he said.

"Okay." Zulema looked up. "Shh. She's coming."

The girl set their drinks and pastries on the table. "Will there be anything else?"

Bevon smiled, and this young girl sighed. Really? The sad part was that Derrick Valoric wasn't a particularly good-looking guy, which begged the question: why would a princess want to give up everything to be with him? Unless Tamarella hoped he'd move to Feyrion. But to what end? He was a warlock just like Tristan—unless Derrick was far more powerful.

Zulema looked up. "Yes. Do you remember Tamarella ever coming in here?"

"Oh, yes. Not often, mind you, but a few times. She either came in with her cousins or her mate. Mostly her mate in the last few months." She leaned closer. "Did you meet the cousins yet?" The girl practically giggled.

"Bevon and Kenton?"

"Yes. Kenton, who is the old brother is a bit too reserved for me, but his younger brother? Oh, my." Her eyes lifted to the ceiling as she sighed.

Bevon leaned back in the seat with a rather smug look on his face. "Is that so?"

"Yes. He was really nice, and he tipped good, too."

Zulema didn't need to hear how he had the locals swooning, nor did they need him to give away his real identity. "To answer your question, I have not met either brother. They weren't here when I visited before. Can I ask if when you saw her, did Tamarella seem happy?"

"For the most part. I mean, the man she was to mate with was also very good looking, so there was no reason not to be happy."

"Better looking than her cousins?" Bevon asked.

She shook her head. "Oh, no."

Zulema had had enough and kicked him under the table. Bevon shot a quick glance at her, clearly enjoying having his ego stroked.

"Back to my friend. When you heard she committed suicide, what did you think?" Zulema asked.

"I couldn't believe it. She was a princess. She had everything to live for."

Money didn't necessarily bring happiness. "Besides me, did anyone else come in and ask about the family?"

Their server looked over at Bevon. "Just you," she said to him.

His mouth slightly parted. "When was this?" Zulema asked, not wanting Bevon to slip up.

"It was one month ago."

He nodded. "That sounds about right."

"You, too, wanted to know how to find where the princess lived," the server said.

"That's because it was my first time here." Thankfully, he sounded quite convincing.

"Are you sure about the date?" Zulema asked. How could a waitress remember who came into a coffee shop a month ago?

"Very sure. It was my birthday, and I thought the gods had answered my prayers to bring me a rich and handsome man." Her face turned red. "I'm so sorry. I didn't mean to be forward."

"It's okay. We're not together." Zulema wasn't with Derrick Valoric, and she didn't need the world to think otherwise.

"Oh."

"Do you remember anyone else coming here to ask for directions?" Zulema asked.

"There are always tourists, but they just like to look at the outside of the castle."

Zulema glanced at Bevon to see if he had any other questions.

"What's your name?" he asked.

Zulema wanted to kick him again.

"Ceylon."

"Well, thank you, Ceylon, for the information."

"Just ask if you want to know anything else."

She nodded, turned around, and left. Once she was back at the counter, Zulema leaned on her elbow and partially covered her mouth. "What do you think?"

"My mother told me the same thing about Derrick."

"She knew he was here?"

"Yes. How else would she know what he looked like?"

Zulema had wondered about that. "Did your mom say if he was angry that his mate was to be…given to another man?"

"I didn't ask her about his state of mind, but I will."

"Do you know why he came here? I thought Tamarella didn't talk about him to her family."

He smiled. "I don't know. Just so you are not confused, Derrick didn't come knocking on my mother's door. My mom was with her sister at the time. I think Derrick said he wanted to say goodbye or something."

"I'm betting he either wanted to get the lay of the land or wanted to try to convince your cousin to change her mind about being with Tristan."

"All of that is possible," he said.

He wasn't helping. "Does this point the finger at Derrick or away from him?"

"Hard to say. If he was here, he might have tried to talk my cousin into returning with him. If she said no, he might have become angry."

"I agree with the angry part, but why not kill Tristan to pave the way for Tamarella to be with him?"

His eyebrows rose. "You know, you should consider a career change."

What did that imply? "To what? I'm a damn fine bodyguard."

He held up a hand. "To being a private investigator."

"Oh." Zulema had to admit this was getting her blood pumping. "I'll think about it—assuming we can solve this case in another week."

"I love your attitude. What's next on the agenda, detective."

"Funny. We should talk to Tristan, though if he sees you—or rather who he thinks you are—he might not be very hospitable."

"True, but I doubt he'd make a scene in front of the staff—or you."

"I wonder why Tristan isn't investigating Tamarella's death?" Zulema asked.

Bevon polished off his drink. "Excellent question. Maybe we should ask him."

Chapter Nineteen

"DO YOU THINK this is a good idea?" Zulema asked. Meeting with Tristan at his home was like purposefully walking into the opposition's locker room.

"I've known him for much of my life. Tristan is harmless," Bevon said.

Harmless as a murderer.

"Master Tristan will be right down," the butler said.

This home was not nearly as grand as either Bevon's family estate or the one Tamarella lived in, but it was still lovely.

Tristan came down the hallway and halted. "You!"

Bevon held up his hand. "I just want to talk. I need to find out who killed Tamarella."

"It wasn't you?"

Oh, shit. Did he know it was Bevon?

"Me?" Bevon asked. "Tamarella was *my* mate. Why would I harm her?"

"I don't know. I've been going crazy trying to figure it out. I know it wasn't suicide," Tristan said. "Tamarella loved life."

If Tristan believed that, he should be pounding the streets looking for her killer—or demanding the medical examiner re-examine the body. In truth, she had no idea if Feyrion even performed autopsies.

Tristan turned his back and led them toward a parlor where they all sat down. "You're positive she didn't take her life?" Zulema asked.

His brows scrunched. "Who are you again?"

She hadn't said. Zulema inhaled. "I'm Anna DeLeon."

His eyes widened. "Tam's friend from Tarradon?"

Zulema wasn't sure how much Bevon's cousin had revealed to this man. "Yes."

"You must be upset by her death, too."

"I am. Totally. I had no idea she had passed until after I arrived here."

Bevon leaned forward, planting his elbows on his knees. "Why do you think Bevon killed her?"

She was thankful to have that line of questioning discontinued.

"Bevon? Are you crazy? He didn't kill her. What gave you that idea?"

Oh, shit. Good luck answering that one, Bevon.

"I heard that you accused Bevon of the crime."

Tristan stabbed his fingers through his short dark hair. "I sent you a note saying that Tam was dead. That's all." He stilled. "William did give you that note, right?"

"Yes. William, the rather short man with sandy blond hair."

"That's him."

She had to assume Bevon was aware of the staff at Tristan's home. "Could he have written his own note for some reason?" Zulema asked.

"Why would he?" Tristan looked back at Bevon. "I know Tam loved you and not me, but we had a plan. You know it."

Okay, this was news. "What plan?" she asked, fearing Bevon wouldn't have any idea how to answer.

"Tam didn't tell you?"

Zulema could feel herself sinking. "No. It's not something we discussed."

"Your best friend should have let you in our little deception." Tristan waved a hand. "On the surface, we would be the loving couple. But...I had no problem with her portalling back to Tarradon to be with Derrick."

Zulema had to work hard to keep her emotions in check. "You were okay with that?"

"Yes. I'm in love with Betina, but my parents wouldn't allow us to be together."

Betina? Interesting that the handmaiden left out that tidbit of information. The fact his parents would dictate who he could or couldn't be with was a bit sad. "I see."

Bevon crossed his arms. "I thought the plan was rather foolproof, but then someone killed her."

Zulema wanted to settle this suicide thing once and for all. "Other than not believing Tamarella would have taken her life, how are you so sure she was murdered?" She directed her question to Tristan.

"I personally am not affected by treniam, but Tam explained to me what would happen if someone rubbed it on her. Her heart rate would skyrocket, and then her muscles would lock up. Even if she had been able to cut her wrists, I believe the blood would coagulate before she had the chance to bleed out."

"What are you saying?" Bevon asked.

"I don't think she died from blood loss. I think someone used the treniam to paralyze her, and then he—or she—poisoned her. It's the only thing that makes sense."

"What about the slit wrists?" Zulema asked.

"That was probably done afterward to make it look like suicide. Betina said there wasn't a lot of blood."

"That's not what she told me," Zulema said.

"I think she's had time to think about things. I don't fully understand a Fairy/Fey's constitution to know how much she would bleed in that case."

"What did the autopsy say?" Zulema couldn't help but dig deeper.

Tristan's lips pressed together. "There wasn't one."

Since he seemed to know the word, she bet they had them here. "Why not?"

"Her father refused, saying he didn't want anyone to cut up his daughter."

"I can understand that, but surely he'd want to know the truth."

"What would be the point? His daughter would still be dead," Tristan said.

Really? That was not a good answer, but it wasn't her place to say so. "I see." Zulema inhaled. "What about your brother?"

"Carmen? What about him?"

"Would he want to harm her?" she asked.

Tristan stood. "No, now please leave. And don't come back. Either of you."

Temper, temper, though he probably had a right to be upset. Bevon clasped her wrist, and they disappeared a second later. She hoped that Derrick could teleport. Otherwise, Bevon might have just blown his cover.

They appeared in his cabin on Feyrion. "We need to return to Tarradon," he announced with such seriousness, it almost scared her.

"Why?"

"We need to talk to Derrick."

He'd lost his mind. "For starters, we'd have to find him. Secondly, why would he talk to you? You're supposed to be dead."

"Not as myself or Derrick. I'll have to change my appearance again."

She hoped she could still see the original Bevon after the change. Knowing who he was and seeing a different face and body creeped her out a bit. "What would you say to him?"

"I want to find out if the message he received from this William guy only claimed that Tam was dead. Tristan might be lying."

"What if he says it said something else—that you, Bevon Forrester, killed her?" She didn't see what this would accomplish. They couldn't trust Derrick to tell the truth.

"I'll ask to see the note."

Zulema blew out a breath, needing him to realize this wouldn't work. "What if he says he doesn't have it?"

"Then I'll find William."

He seemed to have an answer for everything. "Do you even

know this messenger's last name?"

Bevon's jaw tightened. "No." He looked at the ground for a moment. Most likely he was soliciting help from one or more family members to find out. He nodded. "I should know that information shortly."

"Nothing stops you, does it?"

Bevon looked up at her, and the tension from a moment ago disappeared. In its place was lust. He moved closer. "Not when I want something."

The glint in his eyes implied he wanted her. "Do we have time?" He needed to have his face changed, and then they had to find Derrick.

He laughed. "When my princess has sex on her mind, we'll make the time."

That would be insulting if it weren't true. "You can't tell me you aren't interested."

He grinned, and her pulse fluttered. "I'm always interested. We are mates after all."

Her heart dropped to her stomach. So what if one of the women from the pottery shop said the same thing—or had it been Tory? Too much had happened to keep things straight.

"We are." Zulema was proud of herself for remaining so calm.

"I can't tell you how happy I am to hear that." Bevon clasped her by the waist and drew her near.

Zulema expected a toe tingling kiss, but instead, he ran gentle kisses down her neck, causing goose bumps to rise on her arms. The sensuality and luxury of it made her fall a little bit more in love with him. Never did she think she'd meet a man who fit her needs so perfectly—but now she had. The fact he was a prince didn't really affect her, but it was nice that he was so well connected.

Needing to enjoy him more fully, Zulema slid her hands under his shirt and was thrilled to feel his flexing muscles. How much was he making them move on purpose, versus how much those bulges were moving naturally, was anyone's guess. Regardless, his body did something to her. All she could say was thank goodness he looked like the Bevon she knew and not like Derrick Valoric.

His erection pressing against her jarred her a bit out of her daydream, creating so many sparks of strong need that desire scattered all over her body. With each kiss, his arms and chest glowed brighter and brighter white.

Zulema leaned her head back, exposing more of her neck. "Your light is growing. Does this mean you're excited?" She knew the answer but wanted confirmation.

"Why don't you touch me and find out?"

She laughed, loving that idea. Instead of letting him take the lead this time, she teleported them to the bedroom. They landed on the bed with him on his back. "Much better. How about taking off your shoes and only your shoes?"

"Are you planning on removing the rest one piece at a time?" He grinned.

"Absolutely."

Bevon swiped his hand to remove his shoes and then leaned back on his elbows. "Let the show begin."

He sure was ripe for plucking. "Oh, my. I have so much to choose from! Where should I begin?"

"Take your pick."

Zulema straddled him, unbuttoned his jeans, and tugged. She had to move in order to finish taking them off though. When she saw he wasn't wearing anything underneath, tingles of excitement stirred her. "I like that you went commando."

He grinned. "I thought it would be easier for you."

It wouldn't have been an issue at all if he'd swept a hand to take off his clothes. "I appreciate that."

"Your turn."

Shit. She'd forgotten about that. Sitting on the bed, she ditched her shoes and then slipped off her pants. She left her panties on, as well as her top. Having Bevon remove them might be more fun.

"Nice." Bevon ran a finger under the elastic of her panties, and her skin heated. The electricity charging through her body made Zulema wiggle her hips.

"My turn again," she announced. Any more of his touches and she'd have to ask him to swipe off their clothes so they could indulge in her next fantasy right away.

He didn't listen to her request. Instead, he pulled her to his chest and kissed her. Hard. With dominating passion. Zulema gave in and let her hands roam where they wished. His long, silky hair slid through her fingers. Only when she lowered her palms to his face, did the change in texture register. The slight cheek bristle was a turn on.

To hell with taking off the rest of their clothes. He could use his magic if he wanted. Only he didn't. Bevon never ceased to surprise her.

He slipped his hands under her shirt and lifted the material. "Raise your arms," he said. She wasn't going to argue. In a second, her shirt was history. "Bras suck."

She laughed, and then it was gone. Two could play at this game. "So does your t-shirt."

"Is that so?" Poof. Shirt gone. Where it went, she didn't know, nor did she care.

Bevon rolled her onto her back and then slid down between her legs. The anticipation alone had her soaring. When he widened her legs and swiped a tongue across her sensitive nub, she debated dragging his face to hers and biting him on the neck. They were mates, but she didn't want to rush the emotional connection, even though they had the physical connection down pat.

In between licks, he slipped two fingers into her opening and found her sweet spot in seconds. Zulema pressed her feet against the mattress and lifted her hips, yearning for more pressure. Heat built inside of her.

This is amazing, her dragon panted. *Bite him now.*

Zulema didn't have time to debate the timing of their mating, so she didn't respond. What she wanted was Bevon's cock—any way she could get it. He wiggled his fingers back and forth, eliciting wave upon wave of erotic lust. As much as she wanted him to plunge into her, she wouldn't beg. At least not yet. Bevon continued teasing and tempting her, seemingly to need the release from all that happened today.

Bevon reached up and brushed his palm against a sensitive nipple, and her body caught fire at the intimate touch.

"Harder," she cried out.

"Easy, princess. You'll get what you want in a moment."

Bevon returned to frustrating and exciting her. Each swipe sent shards of joy racing up her spine, forcing her to grab his shoulders. As much as she tried not to let her orgasm take over so quickly, when he drew her tiny nub into his mouth and flicked his tongue over her clit, Zulema lost control. Her climax swooped in and claimed her.

Her breath whooshed out. "Incredible," was all she could manage to say.

"I have a lot more in store for you."

Keeping his gaze on her face, he elbowed his way up to her. As soon as his lips were close to hers, he slid into her wet opening. Joy surrounded her, as did his white glow. Her nails sharpened as the heat inside her fired up again.

His kisses ignited her desire, and Zulema met his thrusts with equal fervor. Careful to avoid breaking skin, she dug her nails into his shoulders, never losing contact with his luscious lips.

Bevon grunted, and when his eyes flashed gold, he looked like a god. The harder he hammered into her, the higher she soared. Her world spun, and she ceased to think of anything but the incredible joy this man brought to her life.

Bevon broke the kiss, sucked in a big breath, and drove in once more. When he closed his eyes and opened his mouth, Zulema came with the intensity of a hurricane.

A few seconds later, Bevon followed, his cock pulsing and throbbing. What happened after that was a bit unclear. She awoke all snug in the bed with Bevon smiling down at her.

"What happened?" she asked.

"I tired you out. Get up. Time for my makeover."

Chapter Twenty

W HILE BEVON WAS working with his mother to create a new persona, Zulema teleported outside to the garden. Arianna had told her that Zulema's mom was going a bit stir crazy and asked to be allowed to explore the grounds.

When Zulema spotted her mother leaning over some flowers and smelling them, her heart swelled. How was this possible? Every doctor claimed her mother's condition was fatal. Never did Zulema expect to see her up and about again.

"Mom?" Zulema called. Her mother spun around, smiled, and waved. Zulema jogged over to her. "You look positively radiant."

Her mother hugged her. "It's a miracle. I can't thank you enough for bringing me here. The medical staff is exceptional."

Bevon's mom didn't work for anyone. "Maybe we could sit down. I have some explaining to do."

Arm in arm, they sauntered over to a bench that was surrounded by richly colored and fragrant flowers, most of which Zulema couldn't identify. She inhaled. "I love the smell of roses."

Her mother tucked in her chin. "Roses? They most certainly are gardenias. I should know. Those are my favorite flowers."

And roses were Zulema's favorites. Was it possible the scent was tailored to each person? Given what Bevon could do, Zulema was starting to believe anything was possible in Feyrion. "Maybe they are."

"Tell me how you found this place. I didn't see any other patients."

Oh, my. This would take some work. Now that her health was

on the mend, Zulema didn't want to lie anymore. "This is someone's home."

"A home? It's so big."

"The woman who treated you is the queen of this realm."

"This realm? We're not on Tarradon? Are you saying we're on Earth?"

Zulema inhaled. This might be more difficult than she thought. "No, not Earth. It all started when someone kidnapped me."

Her mother sucked in a breath. "What! Why?"

For the next twenty minutes, Zulema detailed her agreement with Derrick and how she ended up falling in love with Bevon. "I know, I know, it was wrong on every level to agree to take another person's life, but I couldn't let my captor kill you and Maylora. In the end, everything turned out okay." She explained about Bevon faking his death.

"Then why hasn't your sister been freed?"

Zulema was happy that her mother could follow the series of events enough to realize what had transpired. "That is what Bevon and I are about to find out. For now, she and Aislin are safe and hidden in a home somewhere." Zulema held up a hand. "Don't ask about my source. It's complicated." No one could comprehend Fairies disintegrating into points of light unless they'd seen it with their own eyes. "Bevon and I are going to talk to Derrick to see why he is still holding them captive."

"But he'll see Bevon isn't dead."

She explained about his mother's ability to change his looks. "It will be okay. Bevon is far more powerful than Derrick. Nothing bad is going to happen."

Just because the warlock could take away her powers for as long as he desired, it didn't mean he could do the same to Bevon. Even Derrick seemed afraid of him. Bevon was a Fey, after all.

Her mother clasped her hand. "This worries me that something will happen to you."

Zulema figured her mother would respond that way. "I will be fine. I have Bevon."

"Where is this man? I want to meet him."

Her mother had met him when Bevon carried her here. Mom must have forgotten. "He's putting on his disguise for when we meet Derrick. He'll stop by here soon."

Her mom's smile appeared briefly. "If you're happy, so am I, but be careful. I would die if I lost you."

"Don't worry." Or were those famous last words?

Bevon appeared a few feet from them and smiled. Thank goodness his looks hadn't changed to her. "How did it go?" Zulema asked.

"My mother made me ugly."

Zulema laughed, but when she looked over at her mom, her turned down lips implied he was right. Bevon did seem to take pride in his good looks. "Now you get to see how the other half lives," she said to him.

"As if you know."

Her mother stood and held out her hand. "Thank you for everything. You saved my life."

"My mom actually saved you."

Her mother looked over at Zulema. "But you saved my daughter, too."

"Zulema saved herself, but I'd like to help your other daughter next. For that to happen, Zulema and I need to leave."

"Of course." Her mom turned and hugged her. "Hurry back."

"We will."

Zulema pressed her communication bracelet to her chest to activate it. *"Where to first?"* she telepathed.

"I've asked Fay and Meena to confirm that Derrick lives where Logan claims. We'll stop by the cabin first and move on from there."

She loved that he wasn't going to wing it. Derrick Valoric was a dangerous man and needed to be treated with caution.

Once on the front lawn of the castle, Bevon made his usual portal, and seconds later, they were inside his Tarradon cabin. It was almost like home sweet home.

He pressed a hand to his ear. A second later, his two sisters appeared. "How did it go?" Meena asked.

The strange part was she didn't act surprised by Bevon's new look, not that Zulema could see it. Maybe Fairies were immune to facial changing too.

"Did you check the address I gave you for Derrick Valoric?" Bevon asked. "We want to speak with him. Now."

"We did. He's home—or he was a few minutes ago. But what do you hope to gain?"

Bevon explained about Tristan's claim that he never said anything about Bevon being Tamarella's killer.

"Then why did Valoric commission Zulema to kill you?" Fay asked.

"That is what we'd like to find out," he said.

"You believe he'll tell you the truth?" his older sister asked.

"I won't know unless I confront him. It's not as if he can harm me."

Zulema was thankful for that.

"How about we take you there? You know I'm not good at giving directions. Once we arrive, Meena and I will check up on Zulema's sister and her friend to make sure Valoric doesn't issue some kind of kill order."

Zulema's heart plummeted to her chest. Bad news rarely affected her when she was in her bodyguard mode, but when it came to her family, she was way too sensitive.

"I appreciate that." He looked over at Zulema. "You okay with that plan? I know you'd rather free them first, but I think this is the better approach."

She was stinging from the idea that Derrick would harm her family even after she'd, in theory, killed Bevon. "I am. Do you think I should carry the medallion? If I don't have it, I fear he'll wonder what I've done with it—or realize that I know it has a tracking device on it."

"Definitely take it. You might even be able to use it as a bargaining chip. The medallion for your family."

"Wouldn't that be nice? It's back at my house."

"Let's get it."

Bevon and Zulema clasped hands with the two sisters. A second later all four of them were in Zulema's house. "I'll be just a second."

Once she retrieved it from the deep recesses of her closet, they teleported again to a rather nice neighborhood. This wasn't the house where her sister and Aislin were being held, but that was okay. Zulema was confident she could get Derrick to release them—even if she had to promise to do more work for him—not that she would, but he didn't have to know that.

"We'll make sure Zulema's family is safe. I don't trust the Zon not to move them every few days."

She loved how concerned they were. "Thank you."

The two sisters disappeared. She was sure they would communicate telepathically if the situation changed.

Bevon faced her. "How about we pretend to be involved romantically?"

That came out of the blue, despite it being true. "Why?"

"At some point I might ask to be exchanged for your sister and your friend. If he thinks I am important to you, he might be willing to make the trade."

While she loved her sister more than anything, it wouldn't be fair to ask Bevon to do that. "No!"

He grinned. "It's not like he can take my powers away. I'll just teleport out of there if he locks me in a room. If he manages to curb that talent, trust me, I have an arsenal of them."

"Good to know, but let's hope it doesn't come to that. Since I kind of work for him—in a perverted sort of way—let me start the conversation."

"Sounds good."

They hadn't worked out all of the logistics. "What is your name? I can't call you Bevon or Derrick."

"What would you like it to be, princess?" Bevon never stopped being the carefree spirit.

"I do love your name, but for obvious reasons, that wouldn't work. How about Brock Rickart?"

He laughed. "Wherever did you get that name?"

It would be embarrassing to tell him she'd found some silly romance book written by an author on Earth, and that hero was named Brock. "I made it up."

"Brock it is."

She could do this. Zulema just had to think of this as another assignment.

"One other thing," she said. "We shouldn't show him you have any abilities. You should pretend to be an ordinary human. Derrick won't think to remove powers you don't have."

His eyes widened as he hissed in a breath. "Even I don't think I'm that good of an actor."

He was kidding, so she punched his arm. "You are too. Come on."

They walked the last few hundred feet to the front of the house. She knocked, hoping Derrick would answer even though he hadn't responded to her call. Most likely there were cameras pointed at them, so she hooked her arm around Bevon's.

After a long wait, someone answered, but he didn't look like the man Bevon had mimicked. This man was several inches over six feet, bald, with a lot of muscles. Bodyguard would be her guess.

"What do you want?" the gruff man asked.

"I'm Zulema Garcia. I've completed a job for Mr. Valoric and would like my compensation."

The man nodded to Bevon. "Who's he?"

She was so tempted to say he was the man she was sent to kill, but that would be stupid. "He's my boyfriend, and he insisted on coming with me." She rolled her eyes, trying to stay in character. "Not that he would stand a chance against someone like you."

Sure, she'd poured it on a little thick, but having worked with many other male bodyguards, she understood their big ego.

"Come this way."

Yes! Now came the hard part.

The bald bodyguard led them down a hallway. At the end, he knocked.

"Come in."

That voice. It gave her the chills. She casually pressed the bracelet to her chest. *"That's him."*

The guard pushed open the door, and they stepped inside. The room was nothing like the opulent office she'd been taken to during her captivity. This one was more modern and didn't have some fancy bar. Interesting.

Even though she'd seen what Derrick looked like for a small window of time when Bevon had his looks, seeing Valoric in person unnerved her. Since she'd completed the mission—as far as Derrick was concerned—she had no reason to believe he would try to take away her powers again.

"Ms. Garcia. How nice to see you again."

The man was full of shit. "Why is that?"

"To thank you, of course, for doing what I asked."

Relief filled her, but it was hard to shutter her revulsion for this man. "I did."

He motioned they take a seat. Once on the sofa, Bevon grabbed her hand, clearly wanting to establish he was a dear and protective boyfriend.

"I don't think I've had the pleasure of meeting your companion. In fact, I wasn't aware you had a mate."

At least she didn't have to lie this time. "You never asked. Perhaps you need to punish those who provide you with faulty information."

He smiled, but it was anything but sincere. "I guess I shall. I trust you are here to demand the release of your sister and friend?"

She swallowed her anger. "It's hardly a demand. More like collecting on a promise."

He leaned back in his seat. "I will in due time."

What a fuck. Of course, he wouldn't just release her family. She was good at her job, and no doubt he'd demand more from her. It would never end unless she and Bevon did something.

Bevon squeezed her hand. "Zulema told me about your deal."

"I'm surprised. Most people don't like to admit they are assassins."

"Be that as it may, while Zulema didn't seem to mind killing someone who might have been innocent…"

Derrick's eyes widened. "Innocent? That's a laugh. I was told in no uncertain terms that a man by the name of Bevon Forrester killed my mate."

"In no uncertain terms? What exactly did that mean?" Bevon asked, his voice sharp.

Derrick pulled out a desk drawer and retrieved a piece of paper. "The man my Tamarella was to *join with* told me who killed her. Here's the proof."

He handed the note to Bevon who read it out loud. "I know who killed Tam. It was Bevon Forrester. Signed Tristan." Bevon whistled. "I guess that proves it." He gave the paper back to Derrick. "You're certain this Tristan person didn't lie? Maybe he killed her."

Derrick shook his head. "I've met Tristan. He and I had an understanding. While he might have been her mate in public, Tam and I would be mates in the truest sense."

The grief in his voice was real. Too bad he'd been misinformed.

"Did Tristan himself deliver the message?" Zulema asked, knowing full well he hadn't.

"No, some kid brought it here."

"A kid?" Bevon asked.

"Yes, why?"

"I'm sure it's nothing," she said. "When I visited Feyrion—thanks to the medallion you gave me—I too spoke with Tristan. Not that I didn't believe Bevon wasn't guilty, but I'm the thorough type."

"I know," Derrick said. "It was one reason why we picked you."

We? That implied the Zon organization had a hand in this. "Tristan said he asked an older man, by the name of William, to deliver a note to you."

"I wouldn't know about that. What did Tristan say the note contained?"

"It merely stated that Tamarella had died. He never said who he thought had killed her. Everyone had been led to believe she committed suicide." She almost smiled when his face paled.

"That's a lie," Derrick said. "You read the note. It said Forrester killed Tam."

"Why would Tristan lie?" she asked, trying not to defend Bevon.

"I don't know. I was under the impression that he wanted this union as it would strengthen his family's coffers. I guess I misjudged Tristan."

"Perhaps someone else killed her," she said.

"That may be, but who? I haven't been to Feyrion in a while. Maybe you can find out for me. Yes, that's it. You've done an excellent job so far."

She barked out a laugh. "I killed Bevon for you—an innocent man. That should be enough."

It wasn't as if he didn't have other assassins at his beck and call. Hadn't he hired the man to shoot an arrow into Bevon's back?

Valoric dragged a hand down his cleanly shaven face. "I'm sure you don't think much of me, but I don't kill people on a whim. I wanted revenge against the person who murdered the woman I loved. If what you say is true, the killer is still out there."

"It's not my concern."

Bevon stood. "We are done here. Release Zulema's sister and friend. Now."

She loved the authority in his voice, but she doubted Derrick cared.

"And if I don't? What will you do?" Derrick asked with annoying arrogance.

Chapter Twenty-One

D ERRICK'S QUESTION WAS a good one. What would Bevon do if Valoric didn't return Zulema's family? Bevon had to respond as if he were an ordinary human, even though that was a concept he was unfamiliar with.

What he wanted to do was strangle this man, retrieve Maylora and Aislin, and return to his peaceful life with Zulema by his side. The problem with that was that he, too, didn't kill indiscriminately. Most likely, if he harmed Derrick Valoric, the Zon would come after Zulema and kill her this time.

"We'll tell everyone what and who you are," Bevon said. He almost laughed at his weak threat.

Derrick's brows rose. "Is that so? I'd like to see how far you get with that. The authorities would throw your girlfriend in jail for murdering Bevon Forrester."

Bevon wasn't about to say that couldn't happen, because there was no body. "I have an idea."

Derrick tilted his head. "Oh, this should be rich. Tell me."

"Take me as prisoner instead of Aislin and Maylora."

"Why would I do that? I've dampened their powers, not that I know if Aislin even has any."

Zulema took a step forward. "Because this man means more to me than anyone." She looked over at him. "I love Brock."

What Bevon wouldn't give to hear her say that using his name instead. "What do you say, Valoric?"

"Let me think about it."

That would give Bevon time to find the real messenger, though he had a feeling the man did not end up in a good place. "Come on, sweetheart. Let's give this man some space."

She pulled out her medallion. "I assume you want this back?"

Derrick held up a hand. "Not yet. Knowing your curious mind, you might be tempted to find the person who really killed Tamarella. Do that and I will be in your debt. Contact me when you learn something."

Bevon hoped she wouldn't laugh in Valoric's face. "In the meantime, what about my family?" she asked.

"I will treat them like I would my own sisters."

He doubted that. "Let's go, Zulema."

The same bodyguard escorted them out. As tempted as Bevon was to teleport, he had to remember he had no powers. But Zulema did. "How about we go back to your place?"

"Why not your cabin?" she asked once the bodyguard returned inside.

"Derrick might be monitoring us. In theory, you were at my cabin to seduce me before you killed me. There would be no reason for you to return."

She tapped her temple. "I like a man with a clear head. I'm still thinking about my sister and friend, I guess."

She grabbed a hold of him and teleported them back to her place, landing in the middle of her living room. Zulema inhaled. "It's stuffy in here."

Bevon waved a hand and infused fresh air along with the scent of frenlan.

Zulema grinned. "That is incredible."

He loved that her eyes grew wide. Bevon brushed his chest with his knuckles like he'd seen some on Earth do. "Aw, shucks, darlin'. It was nothing."

She laughed. "You sound so…"

"Earthly?"

"Yes."

"Let me ask my sisters to come here." He glanced downward and then nodded. "They'll be here in—"

Before he could finish his sentence, both Meena and Fay appeared. "How did it go?" Meena asked.

"About as well as could be expected," he said. "Valoric didn't have any idea who I was, so that part was good."

"Bevon offered to trade himself for my sister and Aislin."

Meena looked distraught, but Fay was her usual stoic self. "Since you are here, brother, I'm assuming he turned you down?" Fay asked.

"He's thinking about it. Did you find out anything about William, the messenger?" he asked.

"His name is William Belchek from Grindale Province."

Bevon waited for an address or whether he was alive, but Fay said nothing. Sometimes, he wanted to strangle her too. "Is he alive?"

She looked over at Meena. "We think so."

"Can you find out?" Zulema asked.

"There are some things we can't do. I suggest you use conventional methods to find him."

"Can you tell me if Maylora and Aislin are still safe?" Zulema asked.

"We just saw them. They are good, but we'll head back there now to make sure they remain well," Fay said.

Then both of his sisters disappeared. "That was rather passive-aggressive, wasn't it?" he commented.

She grabbed his hand. "Did I embarrass them?"

Bevon pulled her into his arms. "No. To this day, there are things about my family I don't understand. Hell, I don't think even they understand what they can and can't do." He tapped her nose. "Never fear, I have a plan."

She smiled. "If you ever had a gravestone, which I know you'll never have, it would say I have a plan."

He cracked up. "I do adore you."

She cupped his face. "And I you."

"Is that so?"

Zulema pushed back on his chest. "We can't keep getting distracted. We have to find William. I'm guessing he'll be honest about whether Derrick or Tristan was telling the truth."

"My money is on Tristan."

"Mine too, though both might be. We know there is a killer on the loose. Tristan gave the letter to William, and yet a young boy delivered a different one. I'm thinking the killer wanted to give Derrick the wrong message, so he'd put a price on your head."

Bevon stepped back. "You're right." Bevon paced a bit. "Instead of Derrick wanting me dead, it might be someone else. But who?"

"The killer isn't powerful enough to go after you himself, so he thought if Derrick hired me, I could seduce you—and then kill you."

"And you did. Bewitch me, that is."

Zulema fought a smile. "We need to be serious. Who hates you that much?"

"No one. I'm loved by all."

Her shoulders lowered as she let out a breath. "You need to take this seriously. Someone, who doesn't want to be identified, needs you out of the way."

He held up his hands, trying to figure it out in earnest. "There are people who try to enter Feyrion that I've turned down admittance."

"Why don't you want them in your realm?"

"Either they had no reason for entering, or they were from Feyrion originally but were banned due to committing some crime."

"Do you keep a list of these people?"

He tapped his head. "I got it all up here."

"Can you retrieve it from your vast memory?"

"Don't mock." It could take quite a while, but she probably didn't want to hear that. "Our best bet right now might be to find William and ask him, assuming he is still alive. He might know who tried to stop him from delivering the letter to Derrick."

"Good idea. How do we find him? Your sisters didn't give you an address."

"Tory's cousin Logan can find anyone."

She stepped forward, kissed him lightly, and moved back. "What are we waiting for?"

She was a sassy one. Bevon teleported them to Logan's mining office. He wasn't sure if Logan would be in, but he thought Zulema would like to see the Caspian Mining complex anyway.

Zulema grabbed his arm before he walked up to the front door. "Your friend won't know it's you."

"Oh, shit. I forgot I look different. It should be easy enough to convince him. He knows who you are. Tell him who I really am."

"Really? Why would he know me? I've never met the man," she said.

"I might have mentioned you a time or two."

"Really? Why?"

"Remember when Fay first mentioned your name, she thought you were out to harm me?"

Zulema nodded. "And she was right."

"I asked Logan to check you out."

"I remember now. That's when you learned I was an expert with the crossbow and a protector of my family."

"Right." He smiled. "Let's give it our best shot. Okay?"

"Okay."

The woman at the reception desk asked for their names. Bevon decided to go with Brock Rickart. "I'm a good friend of Kenton Forrester."

The receptionist smiled. "Let me see if Mr. Caspian is free." After she contacted him, she stood. "Follow me."

"I've been there before," Bevon said.

The woman's brows pinched. "Then go on back."

Bevon knocked on Logan's door and stepped inside. He placed a hand on Zulema's back and squeezed, indicating she should go first.

She held out her hand. "I'm Zulema Garcia. Bevon said that you would know who I am."

"Briefly. Have a seat."

"I know it is hard to believe because he looks different, but this is really Bevon Forrester."

He chuckled. "Why should I believe you?"

Bevon reminded him of the time his brother had to give Tory a piece of his inner light in order to save her. "If you recall, after he erased her memory, he told you never to tell her."

Logan's mouth opened and then quickly shut. "I'll be damned. Tory mentioned that you were going undercover so that the man who asked Zulema to kill you thought you were dead, but…this?"

Bevon turned his head to the side. "You don't like the new me?"

"No. I hope you can switch back."

"I will when this mess is over."

"What do you need me to do?" Logan asked.

He was happy his friend believed him. "I need you to find a William Belchek." Bevon explained why.

Logan looked up at them. "From what you've said, he might be dead."

"I hope not, but if he is, can you see if his body was picked up by the police and taken to the morgue?"

"You could just call Anderson Caspian."

That was his cousin who was a detective at the Avonbelle Provincial Police Department. "If you can't find William, I will do that."

He supposed he and Zulema could go to town and grab something to eat, but he thought he'd give Tory's cousin a few minutes. In the past, Logan was able to produce miracles quickly.

Less than it would have taken to drink a cup of coffee, Logan leaned back and smiled. The printer shot to life. He grabbed the sheet from the feed. "Here is the address. I even added a map to his location."

Zulema looked over at Bevon and then shot a glance to Logan. "You are amazing. Bevon wasn't exaggerating about your talents."

"I try."

Bevon pushed back his chair and stood. He could have teleported from there, but since Logan couldn't teleport, it would be a little rude. Bevon stuck out his hand. "Always a pleasure."

"Thank you."

He and Zulema left and then teleported to the street where William lived.

"What exactly are you going to ask him?" Zulema questioned.

"I want to establish that he had a message from Tristan to deliver."

"Will you say you're a detective or something?"

"That seems like the best idea." Bevon knocked, but no one answered. "Wait here for a second."

Bevon teleported inside and looked around. The home didn't look as if anyone had been there in a while, mostly because the furniture was covered in sheets. Bevon returned to Zulema. "He's not home." He explained about the covered furniture.

"Maybe one of his neighbors knows if he has any relatives close by. He could be staying with one of them," Zulema said.

He liked that she was able to come up with an alternative solution. "Sounds good."

As they walked next door, a woman came out of the house, wearing a coat, and dangling a set of keys in her hand.

"Excuse me," Bevon called.

"Yes?"

He explained that they were looking for William Belchek. "I'm a friend and have been worried about him."

"I would check with his sister."

Yes! "Do you have an address?"

"I think so. Give me a second." She went inside, and a few minutes later she returned carrying a piece of paper. "Here is the address."

"Thank you."

Not wanting to freak out the neighbor by suddenly disappearing into thin air, they walked down the street, pretending as if they had parked on a side street. When Zulema spotted the neighbor drive by, they teleported close to where the sister lived.

The neighborhood was a lot nicer than the one where William lived. Though if he spent most of his time in Feyrion, it made sense not to spend money on a fancy house.

Bevon knocked, and an older woman answered. "Yes?"

"I'm a friend of your brother's. I need to speak with him. Is he here?"

"Who are you?"

He inhaled. She had to know about Feyrion. "I'm…Kenton Forrester." Bevon didn't look all that much like Kenton even when he had his original face, but she probably wouldn't know that. Now, the two of them were not even close, but if she knew anything about Feyrion, she'd recognize that name.

Her eyes widened, and then she did what looked like a little curtsy. "Come in." They stepped inside. "I'm afraid William was in an accident. He's in bed at the moment."

"What kind of accident?"

Footsteps sounded, and a rather haggard looking man dressed in pajamas padded out. "Who are you?"

It was William. "May we speak? It's about Tristan's note that he gave you to deliver."

His sister rushed up to him. "You shouldn't be out of bed."

"When I heard that Kenton was here, I had to see him. Only this isn't Kenton Forrester."

Well shit.

Chapter Twenty-Two

I T WASN'T RIGHT that Bevon was forced to lie on her account. "We're sorry we deceived you. As you stated, he's not Kenton," Zulema said. "We had to make sure you knew who Kenton was before we could tell you something important."

"Who are you?"

"I'm Zulema Garcia. I worked—against my will, mind you—for Derrick Valoric." When neither William nor Bevon said anything, she rushed on. "He forced me to kill Bevon Forrester."

"You were the one who killed him?" William asked. She nodded. "Get out of my house."

Okay, that wasn't the response she was looking for, but it indicated he was loyal to Bevon's family. Zulema placed her bracelet on her chest. *"How do you want to handle this?"* she telepathed.

Bevon held out a hand. "I know I look different, but I really am Bevon Forrester. Zulema didn't kill me. In fact, she couldn't if she wanted to."

His brows pinched. "Prove you are him."

Bevon disappeared. He then reappeared. "I'm really a Fey."

"A lot of Fey's can teleport. Hell, so can I."

"What would you like to know?" Bevon asked.

"Who is the queen?"

Anyone who'd been to Feyrion could have answered that. "Queen Arianna."

"What is Tristan's family name?" William asked.

"Stanton. Convinced?"

"Let's sit down." He sounded weak, as if someone had stuck a pin in his balloon.

Bevon moved to his side and helped him to a large comfortable looking chair. "Do you want some water?" Bevon asked.

"That would be nice."

Bevon magically created a glass of water, and when he handed it to William, his eyes grew wide. "Mr. Stanton often mentioned how you and your family had many powers. I'm just a servant. I've not seen magic like that."

Zulema was impressed that Bevon and his family didn't go around the realm showing off their powers. "Mr. Valoric told me to kill Bevon—which obviously I didn't—because he received a note from Tristan saying that Bevon had killed Tamarella."

"No, no. That's not what the note said."

Her pulse spiked.

"What did it say?" Bevon asked.

"That Tamarella had died. That's all. There was no mention of Bevon."

"You mean me."

He didn't answer. It was just as well if he didn't believe this truly was Bevon. "Did you deliver the message to Mr. Valoric?" she asked.

He lifted his hand to the back of his head. "I tried, but someone attacked me. When I woke up, I was in a hospital."

His sister came over. "We nearly lost William. The doctors aren't sure what the person used to bash in his head, but my brother ended up with a large gash, along with a serious concussion."

"The headache was the worst of it. I don't know how I'm going to face Mr. Stanton. I failed as a messenger."

"I'll be sure to tell him it wasn't your fault," Bevon said.

While Zulema was sad the man had been harmed, they needed to know who had harmed him. "Did you see who hit you?"

"Yes, but I didn't recognize him."

"Can you describe him?" Zulema asked.

"Young, tall, strong. The usual thug."

Bevon leaned forward. "May I try something? It won't hurt."

"What do you want to do?"

"I'd like to see if I can retrieve that memory. It didn't happen very long ago, so this technique might work."

"If you think it will help."

Bevon knelt down next to William's chair, placed his fingertips on the man's temples, and then closed his eyes. Was he really trying to see into the guy's head? That seemed impossible. Though if the queen could heal Zulema's mother in a short period of time, his family seemed capable of the impossible.

Bevon let go and stood. "I know what the man looks like. I'm not sure how much that will help though. Do you know anything about the Zon?"

"Just what Mr. Stanton warned me about."

"Did Tristan say that Mr. Valoric was a member of this group of warlocks and witches?" Bevon asked.

"He did." He held up a hand. "I swear I was careful. I drove to Mr. Valoric's house, checking to see if anyone followed me. Just as I got out of my car, I was attacked."

"Did you tell anyone you were going there?" Zulema asked.

"No."

"You told me when you came through the portal where you were going," Bevon said.

"Yes, of course, but no one else. Once I arrived on Tarradon, I teleported to my house for a few minutes to make sure the place was still standing. I called my sister to let her know I had arrived safely, and then I drove to Valoric's house. I don't like to teleport on this realm—except when I'm certain no one will notice."

Zulema nodded. "I understand completely. I'm the same way."

"You're a Fey, too?"

"No, but I'm a witch with powers." And a dragon shifter, but she saw no reason to mention that.

Bevon moved back to the sofa. "I wonder how they knew you even had a message from Tristan."

His sister sucked in a breath and moved into the line of sight. "I am so, so, sorry William."

"What did you do?" Instead of being accusatory, his tone was filled with sadness.

"A man came here a few days before you returned. He said he wanted to hire you for a job and asked that if you ever returned to Tarradon—even for a short time—that I should let him know."

"What kind of job?" her brother asked.

"Delivery. It's what you do."

"Did the man give any specifics? Was it to deliver a letter or a package?" Bevon asked.

"No. All he said was once you arrived, I should call him."

"Do you have that number?" Zulema asked.

"I think so." She rushed to get her phone and then did a search. "I have it."

It was probably a throw away phone, but maybe Logan could learn something. "Can you write down the number?"

The sister handed her the information. "I never meant for any of this to happen."

The brother reached out and clasped her hand. "I know you didn't. It was an honest mistake."

Zulema faced William. "How would anyone on Tarradon know you were going to deliver a message from Mr. Stanton to Mr. Valoric?" This implied a mole of some sort.

"I have no idea."

"How often do you come back here?" Zulema asked.

William looked up at his sister. "Maybe four times a year, but it's random."

"To visit or to do work?" she asked.

"A little of both. Mr. Stanton has communicated with Mr. Valoric for a few months now."

Bevon stood. "Thank you for talking to us, but please don't let anyone know I really am alive. That person might take out his revenge on Zulema and her family."

"I promise," William's sister said.

"Never," William added. "Once I heal, I'm heading back to Feyrion. It's a lot safer there."

"Very true," Bevon said. "Don't worry. Zulema and I will deal with the man who injured you."

She wondered exactly what that meant. They thanked both of them for their help and teleported about a mile away.

"What did you think?" she asked.

"About whether I believed them?"

"I guess. Why didn't Derrick say that Tristan's usual messenger didn't arrive?"

"That is an excellent question, princess. We'll need to ask him. Something isn't right about any of this."

"I agree."

"I would say we should march back to Derrick's home and demand answers, but I need some time to think. Are you hungry?" Bevon asked.

"Not particularly, but I wouldn't mind a strong cup of coffee."

"It will probably be safer to find a place outside of Avonbelle Province, where no one knows us."

She liked that idea. "How about I fly us and head east? If we spot a nice town, I'll land, and we can check it out."

"I love it."

He'd not seen Zulema in her dragon form and was anxious to view her in all of her splendor. They teleported to a field where she shifted. Oh my, she was glorious. He'd never seen a purple dragon before. Even her form and size took his breath away.

Zulema held out her claw, and Bevon grabbed hold. It had been a very long time since he'd flown with a dragon. His usual method of transportation was teleporting.

Zulema soared upward, and the sensation of movement—which he didn't experience when teleporting—was thrilling. The landscape fell away beneath them the higher she went. Bevon hadn't realized what he'd been missing all these years. It might even be time to buy a car and drive around to see the beautiful countryside.

Heat from her body balanced the drop in air temperature, and it wasn't long before they spotted a town. Zulema found a field in which to land and began her descent. Darn. When this was over, he'd have to ask her to do this more often.

When she set him down, Bevon's heart continued to race. She stepped back and shifted. He must have looked strange, because she rushed up to him.

"Are you all right?"

"All right? Yes. Yes. That was amazing."

"You haven't flown before?"

She acted as if that was impossible. "Not in a long time and not with you."

His mate stepped closer and cupped his cheek. "That is so sweet." She stood on her toes, and when she kissed him, her stomach grumbled.

As much as he didn't want to break the kiss, he didn't need a hungry woman on his hands. "I think I promised you a meal—or just coffee if that is all you want."

"Thank you. While I would love to have you create another bubble to make us invisible so we can make love in the open air, we have work to do."

He smiled. "Spoilsport."

"Don't worry. I'll make it up to you later."

Bevon grinned, grabbed her hand, and teleported them to a back alley. From there, they cut between two buildings to the main strip. He looked around. "Seems like we have a few choices."

"Let's explore."

It didn't take long before they decided on a seafood place. The inside was rather dark, but that was fine by him. "May we have a booth in back?" he asked.

"Sure."

Once the hostess seated them, he laid out his plan. "We have to find the man who harmed William."

"You don't think he's the killer, do you?"

"No," Bevon said. "Someone would have paid him to knock out William and switch the notes."

"Did you recognize the paper the note was written on?" she asked.

Zulema was sharp. "Yes, which makes me believe this mystery man took the note, copied it somehow, and then changed the wording."

"Is that possible?"

"You should know. We're dealing with warlocks and witches, but I will demonstrate." Bevon picked up a napkin and swiped his hand to create one that looked just like it. Instead of having the logo of the restaurant on it, he changed it to say Zulema and Bevon. That might have been a bit tacky, since it looked like some human wedding invitation, but he had a point to prove. "Voilá."

She studied it. "That is incredible." Zulema leaned closer. "Do you think a Fey or a Fairy is involved?"

That hadn't entered his mind. "Now that you mention it, it's possible a disgraced Fey could be in the Zon."

"William said that not all Feys are equally powerful."

"He's right. We are not all equal. My family has more power than anyone in the realm, because our magic has been passed down for thousands of years."

"I had no idea."

He enjoyed her inquisitive mind. Just as he was about to comment further, their server came over. "Want some wine?" he asked Zulema.

"I think I'll stick to coffee for now."

"Me, too," Bevon said.

He picked up the menu and studied it. Bevon didn't really care what he ate, so he picked a random fish special. "To answer your question about William, all Feys can teleport. Some can make things appear and disappear—like my clothes and the dirty dishes—and some can heal to a limited degree."

"But they wouldn't stand a chance against you in a fight, right?"

"No, they wouldn't. And the average Fey is not immortal." He held up a hand. "That being said, I suppose if a Fey mated with a witch or warlock, their powers would probably combine."

"Good to know what we're up against."

Their server returned, and they ordered. Zulema only asked for a salad. "Your rumbling stomach implied you were hungry."

"I was, but I lost my appetite."

Bevon decided not to push. "Here's my plan. I know what William's attacker looks like. I'll have Logan's cousin, Detective Anderson Caspian, fix me up with a sketch artist. If Anderson can distribute it in the Province, we might get a hit."

"I like that, but you can't draw it?"

He leaned back in his seat. "Princess, I am many things with many talents, but an artist, I am not."

She smiled for the first time in several hours, which did his heart good. "How long do you think that will take?" she asked.

"I'm hoping not long."

Chapter Twenty-Three

A FTER THEY FINISHED their meal, Bevon and Zulema teleported to the Avonbelle Province Police station, but Detective Caspian was not there. Not one to give up, Bevon called Logan and asked if his cousin could meet them. "It's important. And can you explain that I don't look like my usual self."

Logan chuckled. "Can do."

They didn't have to wait at the station for long before the detective arrived. Since Anderson had never met Zulema nor did he recognize Bevon, introductions were needed.

"Anderson, I'm Bevon," he said in a low tone. "I know my face looks different, but there is a reason. Could we go someplace private?"

"Of course. Logan vouched for you. Come this way."

"Thank you. This is Zulema Garcia, by the way. She's part of the reason I'm here."

Edendale was far from where Derrick Valoric resided, but hopefully, even a sketch of William's attacker would help. They entered a small conference room and sat down. "Logan didn't give me much background information."

Bevon started with the death of his cousin on Feyrion. Normally, he wouldn't have told just any detective about this hidden realm, but Anderson Caspian was part of the Guardian family. He just chose to help in a different way from most of the other Guardians. "Because Tamarella's mate was given false information about who had killed her, Derrick Valoric hired—or rather forced—Zulema to kill me."

Anderson looked over at her. "You couldn't go through with it, I see."

"No, but even if I'd wanted to, I couldn't have killed him."

"What do you need from me?" Anderson asked.

"The original messenger was beaten and left for dead. His letter was altered, resulting in Zulema being sent to take me out. I know what this attacker looks like and would like a sketch artist to help."

"I can provide you with one. Anything else?"

"I'm hoping you can give me a name and an address once the sketch is complete." Bevon smiled.

"I'll try." Anderson excused himself.

A minute later, a young man with a computer tablet in hand entered the room. "Shall we begin?"

The process was rather intriguing. Bevon wished he could have swiped a hand and stolen the image from his brain, but it wasn't one of his talents. About thirty minutes later, the artist had come up with a very good likeness. "Excellent work," Bevon said.

The young man barely smiled. "I'll print this off for you and drop it off at Detective Caspian's desk."

Once Bevon received the print out, Anderson scanned the face. "If he has a record anywhere in the province, it should show up." They didn't have to wait long. "We have a match."

"You have a name?"

"Rusty Gerard."

"That's great," Bevon said. "Do you have an address?"

Anderson smiled. "Why, yes I do."

This was their lucky day. After they thanked Anderson profusely, he and Zulema returned to a slightly different part of the province. Unfortunately, the resident thug was not at home.

"What do you want to do?" Zulema asked.

"Normally, I'd suggest we wait here until he returns, but I'm thinking we'd make better headway back to Derrick's house. He lied about not knowing William. What else is he lying about?"

"I don't think he hired Gerard to harm William. Derrick seemed sincere in not knowing that the letter was a forgery."

"I agree, but I will enjoy seeing him squirm," Bevon said.

His mate smiled. "So will I."

Once they were out of view of the good citizens of Edendale, they teleported to Derrick's home. The moment they appeared, however, a sense of foreboding came over Bevon. "Something's not right."

She looked around. "Like what?"

"For starters, the front door is ajar."

"Oh, shit."

They both jogged up to the front, Bevon's senses on high alert. Only a faint sound came from inside. When he pushed open the door, he was met with an obstruction. It was a leg on the ground. With more force, Bevon opened it enough for them to enter. "Derrick's bodyguard."

Blood was pooled around the man's head, presumably from the large gash across his throat.

"That's not good," she said. "I hear something coming from down the hall."

Bevon cloaked himself and then grabbed Zulema's arm to shield her too. He then teleported to Derrick's office. Fuck. As soon as he sensed no one else was there, he reappeared.

Derrick was slouched in his chair with his throat cut, too. Only Derrick was still alive—barely. Bevon was conflicted. Part of him wanted answers, yet the good half said to teleport him to Feyrion where his mother could heal him.

Zulema rushed across the room into what he assumed was a bathroom. She returned with a towel and placed it on Derrick's throat, and applied pressure.

"Who did this?" she asked.

"Rusty...Gerard."

"Why?" she demanded.

"I don't know."

"Who does Rusty work for?" Bevon asked.

Valoric was having a lot of trouble breathing. Even if Bevon did teleport him to Feyrion, the man probably wouldn't live long enough for his mother to treat him. "Peter Delaport."

"Is he Zon?" Zulema asked.

His admiration for his mate grew. It was what he should have asked. Derrick nodded. "Head."

Bevon had never heard of him. "Where can I find him?"

Derrick's body went limp. He was dead. Not good.

Zulema let go of the cloth. "I'm washing my hands."

He had to guess she wasn't used to seeing a lot of death. When she came out of the bathroom, Zulema appeared to be more in control. "You okay?" he asked.

"Yes. I know I should be happy that he's dead, but I can't help but think he was a pawn."

"I have to agree. He loved my cousin. That much was clear."

She blew out a breath and then straightened her shoulders. "I want to save my sister and Aislin now that he can't hurt them anymore." She clasped his arm. "What about Rusty Gerard? Do you think he'll harm them?"

"He may not even know about them. I say we forget about him for now. We have more important things to do. We need to save your family. I'll ask Meena to escort us."

"Thank you," Zulema said.

After he contacted them, Meena appeared. "What happened? Did you do this?"

"If I had been responsible, I wouldn't have used a knife."

She spun around to Zulema who held up her hands. "Don't look at me. I would have shot the bastard in the heart with my crossbow."

Meena smiled. "If you want to free the women, follow me."

They held hands and left. He figured it wouldn't be long before the police found the two dead bodies, and he didn't want to be anywhere near the place.

They arrived in the room where the girls were being held. "Where's the guard?" he asked.

"Don't worry about him. Fay's making sure he doesn't disturb us."

Both women had gags in their mouths and were tied up, but they didn't look abused. With a flick of a hand, Bevon freed them. Joy abound seeing Zulema so happy to be reunited with her sister and friend.

"How did you find us?" Maylora asked.

"Bevon's sisters found you." She nodded to Meena.

A moment later, Fay appeared. *"The guard won't be bothering us or anyone else. I put a shield around the house to keep us from being surprised by any Zon."*

"Thank you," he telepathed back.

Since he and Zulema still had some business to take care of, he figured she'd be more at ease if the women were safe in Feyrion. Most likely he'd have to erase Aislin's memory when she left his realm, but he'd worry about that later.

"Ready to escort the ladies to my place?" he asked.

"Yes," Zulema said with a smile.

They held hands and teleported to his cabin. From there, he created a portal to his home world. He figured if Maylora could see how well her mom was doing, she could relax.

The time of day on Feyrion was different from that on Tarradon. When they arrived, the family was at the dining room table enjoying a meal. The reunion between Zulema's mom and Maylora was worth everything he'd gone through.

"Where is this place?" Aislin asked, her eyes wide with wonder.

"My parents' home." There was no need to mention Feyrion at the moment. "My mother will see you are settled in. Zulema and I will return as soon as we can."

"Thank you so much," Aislin said. She then hugged him.

Maylora spun around. "Did I hear you say that you're both leaving again?"

"I'm afraid so. We have to tie up some loose ends. I promise we'll explain everything the next time we see you."

Zulema and Maylora hugged and said a tearful goodbye.

He tapped his bracelet. *"It's time, Zulema."*

As much as he would have liked to stay, they needed to find either Rusty Gerard or Peter Delaport—preferably the latter—and end this mess once and for all.

Once they were outside, Bevon created a portal and arrived in his backyard in the forest where they teleported inside.

He grabbed Zulema and swung her around. "We did it! Your family is safe."

"Yes and thank you."

He set her down. "What's wrong? I thought you'd be ecstatic."

"I am, but I don't like that someone is still out to get you."

"That is the sweetest thing anyone has ever said to me." Bevon stroked her cheek. "Don't worry. I can take care of myself."

"I know, but you shouldn't have to."

He kissed her quickly. They couldn't afford to dawdle. "How about we take care of Mr. Delaport and then get down to the business of some serious loving?"

Zulema pressed against him. "How serious?"

"The *I love you* kind of serious."

He swore her knees buckled. "I love you back."

"Does that mean what I think it does?" he asked, his eyebrows wiggling.

She stood on her toes and lightly gnawed on his neck. "Yes," she whispered.

Before he succumbed to his needs, he motioned they sit at the kitchen table. "Where do you think we should start?"

"I suppose we could return to Derrick's house and wait for Peter to find you, but that seems a bit reckless."

He chuckled. "Yes. I'd rather surprise him."

"Then why don't we try Logan again? We have the man's name. He can't live too far from Derrick's house."

"It's worth a try. If that fails, if we find Rusty, we'll extract the information out of him."

"Can you make people talk?" she asked.

"That's a loaded question. Let's say, I'm good at *convincing* people. I find magic to be more effective than force."

"I see." She smiled.

It was late, meaning Logan would most likely be at home—enjoying his mate—but as a Guardian, being disturbed at all hours was standard fare. It wasn't as if he hadn't roused Logan out of bed before.

They teleported to his home. "Wait here for a second," Bevon said. "It wouldn't be good to teleport into his house in case Logan and Wendy are doing something personal. I know it bothers me when my sisters do that to me."

Zulema smiled. "It would be a bit embarrassing if we were doing the nasty in the kitchen, and they showed up."

"Exactly."

Bevon cloaked himself and reappeared in the living room. The sound of a television filtered out from the bedroom, implying they were up—or so he hoped. Bevon returned outside. "I'll ring the bell."

A minute later, Logan opened the door. "Hey, what's wrong?"

Why did people always assume the worst? "The man who hired Zulema to kill me is dead."

"Come in. It's a little late to be celebrating though."

Bevon laughed. "The man who commissioned the kill is Peter Delaport. He's the head of the Zon, according to a dying Derrick Valoric."

"And you want me to try to locate him?"

"Yes. I think he's the one who wants me dead. I'm not sure why he killed one of his own, though—or what he has against me, for that matter—but I aim to find out."

"Perhaps you wouldn't let him into Feyrion."

"If that's the case, he's gone to quite a lot of effort to end my life, assuming it is personal."

"Is it possible that Delaport was testing Valoric to see how well he handled a Fey?"

Bevon shrugged. "Anything is possible."

"Follow me into my office. I'll see what I can find."

Bevon and Zulema waited in Logan's office. When Logan returned, he went straight to work. "A man by the name of Rusty Gerard works for him," Bevon said. "I imagine he has a criminal record. They should live relatively close to each other, unless they both can teleport."

Zulema placed a hand on his. "Most of the witches and warlocks I've met can't. My father was an exception."

"Let's hope neither of these men can."

He didn't think now was the time to ask how her father died. He suspected someone had taken away his powers right before his death. The problem with that notion was that it took some fancy spells to block a person's powers. Bevon had done it, but it had only lasted a few minutes. In that case, it had allowed him to defeat his enemy quickly.

"Got something," Logan said.

He and Zulema rushed over. "Is this him?" Logan asked.

The face staring back at him made his blood run cold.

Chapter Twenty-Four

BEVON'S DEMEANOR SCARED her. Zulema had never seen that look before. "Bevon, what is it?"

"He's the man who tried to kill my father. And I stopped him." Bevon visibly shivered.

"Why did he try to kill your dad?" she asked. And wasn't the King powerful enough to stop a warlock? The thought he might not be terrified her.

Bevon stabbed a hand through his hair. "It's not like death threats were foreign to my family, but no one had attacked a family member in hundreds or maybe even thousands of years. This man was a member of the Amalden tribe. They lived on Feyrion and were known for their disruptive behavior—thugs, criminals, thieves. The usual."

"Were they Fey?" It was the only thing that made sense.

"Some were pure Fey, but most—like in the case of this man— were a mix of Fey and Warlock or Witch. His clan believed they should have been the royal ones."

"I didn't think it was something you decided, but rather what the gods decreed," she said.

"Exactly, but the Amalden didn't seem to understand that. They wanted power, and they didn't care who got hurt in their achievement of it."

"They planned to kill your father and take over running the realm?"

"Yes, though if they had succeeded—which would have been slim—it would have moved up the timeline for when Kenton became king."

"They probably assumed that a young man wouldn't be as big a threat as his father. When did this happen?"

He blew out a breath. "Maybe twenty years ago."

"Twenty years? Why wait so long to exact his revenge on you?" she asked.

"Why indeed? Perhaps he didn't know where I was, though I find that hard to believe." Bevon pressed his lips together. "It could have been that he needed to amass his own army of warriors on Tarradon before he tried. When he was expelled from Feyrion, I don't think many went with him."

"Being banned from his home world would have pissed him off." She looked over at Logan. "Were the Guardians aware of the Zon?"

"Their name, yes, but they were never in this part of the province. We aren't the only protectors of the realm, so we never interfered."

"I see." Sort of. "What are you planning to do now?" she asked Bevon.

He stood taller. "I want to confront him, but as my old self."

She could understand that need, even though she didn't like it. Zulema faced Logan. "I trust you have the man's address?"

"I do." He jotted it down and handed it to her.

Bevon seemed to be having some internal battle, and she needed him to focus. "What's next, boss?" she asked Bevon.

He faced her. "Sorry. I need to return to Feyrion and have my mother remove this mask. I plan to show both realms that Bevon Forrester is alive and well."

"You don't think confronting him as Brock Rickart, ordinary human, would be safer? You could surprise him with your magic. I bet he wouldn't see it coming."

He turned to her and cupped her face. "Would you still respect me if I took the cowardly route?"

Her first instinct was to say no, but if this powerful man harmed Bevon in any way, it would kill her. Instead of answering out loud, she placed her wristband to her chest. *"If we mate first, I'll feel a lot better. You might even receive some of my powers."*

"The idea of mating with the woman I love and adore would soothe the beast inside me."

She didn't suggest it might cause him to change his mind. *"Then what are we waiting for?"*

Bevon grinned, and her heart soared.

He faced Logan and held out his hand. "Thank you, my friend. If you ever need anything, let me know."

"I will."

Bevon grabbed her hand and left Logan's home. He then teleported them back to his cabin in the woods. It was late, so spending the night before going into battle made sense.

Zulema expected Bevon to offer her a beer so that they could discuss a plan, but instead he pressed her against the front door and kissed her. No words. No preamble. Just hard core lust oozing out of every inch of his body. The intensity and passion caused her eyes to shut. As much as she loved watching the gold swirls in his eyes, the bright light coming off his body tended to overwhelm her at times.

Any second, Zulema expected him to mentally remove their clothes and teleport them to the bed even though she was perfectly fine right where they were.

The combined pressure on her back and front created both a total calm and a swirling maelstrom of emotions inside of her. Being surrounded by Bevon and everything he represented was where she wanted to be. Forever.

He broke the kiss, and then slid his hands under her shirt. "I love touching you."

"You should be in my body. It's like you're sending pulses of energy through me," she panted.

"That's your trick, my electric babe."

Zulema hadn't meant to bark out a laugh, but that name was too tacky. To show him who he was up against, she reached between them and sent a short burst of power into him.

He jumped back. "I see you found my switch."

She couldn't be more pleased that the Bevon of old had returned. Given their circumstances, that was no small feat. "Is that so? Did I turn you on?"

"You have. And now, it's my turn to do the same to you."

He lifted off her shirt, thrilling her with the way his eyes glazed over. His hands fumbled with unhooking her bra though. So much for being the touted ladies' man.

"To hell with it." In a flash, her bra was nowhere to be seen. "I was never any good with those fancy clasps."

She doubted that, but his magic made things easier. "Works for me."

He drew in a breath as he ran his palms over the tips of her breasts. Bevon certainly seemed to enjoy touching her, but Zulema was definitely the biggest beneficiary.

While she was tempted to run her hands through his hair, she didn't want the distraction, nor did she want to miss one second of this monumental lovemaking. Mating for the first time could only happen once.

Pulses of desire kept exploding inside of her. *"Suck on them,"* she telepathed.

Without using the bracelet, he wouldn't receive the message, but soon…

Bevon swiped a hand and poof, her shoes were gone but not her pants. He must like the seduction part of taking off her clothes one piece at a time. Bevon leaned over and licked one nipple and then the other while he unbuttoned her jeans, and the anticipation caused tingles to pulse between her legs. "Hurry," she begged.

"Let me enjoy this, princess."

"But I need you."

He looked up and grinned. "There are two players here."

From the way his eyes were almost completely gold, he was working hard for control. Wait until it was her turn. She wouldn't play nice until she'd broken him.

Bevon lowered her pants to the ground, leaving on her panties. Seriously? The man was so frustrating. He tapped her leg to indicate she needed to step out of her jeans. First one leg and then the next. At least now, she was almost naked. When it was her turn, she bet he wouldn't be able to resist her for long.

Zulema wiggled her hips, hoping to tempt him further. He grabbed a hold of her to keep her steady, and then planted his face between her legs. Bevon drew in a large inhale, reached up, and palmed both breasts. When he pressed them together, he growled. "You are so amazing."

His desperation ratcheted her desire even more. "Show me."

In one quick move, he tore off her panties, widened her legs, and licked her, causing fire to burst inside of her. Her dragon sure had awoken now.

I'm working hard not to show myself, her inner animal warned her.

Then no mating for you if you don't behave.

Never had her dragon been this excited.

Each lick drove Zulema closer and closer to the brink. Needing to touch him, she reached down and clamped onto his head, careful not to break the skin. She then grabbed his hair and tugged as love and desire swamped her.

When he strummed both of his thumbs over her nipples at the same time he sucked on her clit, she came. Hard. And her yell didn't even sound human.

Bevon sat back on his haunches and smiled.

"See what you did," she said. "I'm done. You lose."

He was on his feet so fast, her head spun. Bevon tickled her until she doubled over with laughter. "Take that back."

She held up a hand. "Okay, okay."

He stopped, pulled her close, and kissed her. His yearning and passion overwhelmed her, but now Zulema needed to return the favor. Instead of teleporting them to the bedroom, she moved them to the sofa. Once he was seated, she immediately straddled him.

"I like the way you think," he said.

"I hope you like what I'm about to do next."

"Bring it on, princess."

Zulema leaned forward and fed him her breast. He fondled and pressed, licked and sucked, until another climax threatened to take hold. She had moved them to the sofa so that she could tempt him, but the opposite had occurred.

Zulema leaned back. "Do that magic thing and take off your pants."

He chuckled. "No. You'll have to work for it."

He was stubborn and unpredictable, but that was part of his charm. Zulema slipped off his lap and pressed on his shoulder so that he was lying flat. She then undid his jeans, walked to the end of the sofa, and tugged.

In a flash, her man was gloriously naked. Just the way she liked him. "Don't move."

"I wouldn't think of it." Bevon grabbed a sofa pillow and placed it under his head.

Now it was her turn to tempt him. She knelt on the floor, leaned over, and licked his rigid cock. Bevon jumped and grabbed her shoulder. "Easy there."

She hadn't even touched him—at least not with her hand. "Be strong, my mate."

"You will pay for that sass."

And she couldn't wait. Being with Bevon was beyond anything she'd ever imagined. He was funny, charming, talented, and so full of magic. But at the moment, she had other things to concentrate on.

She lifted his cock, and ever so slowly, sucked on him. His white glow intensified. When his hard shaft jerked, she stilled. Her goal had not been to make him come—at least not now.

When she started again, his groans got the best of her. The more noise he made, the faster she went until his essence burst inside her mouth. Uh-oh. She swallowed, sat up, and grinned.

"Sorry," she said, even though she really wasn't.

"Don't be." With his gaze on her, he swiped a hand, creating a thick rug next to her. He then eased off the sofa, lifted her up, and gently placed her on her back. A pillow appeared under her head. "Comfy?"

"Yes." Though she'd have made love to him on a hard floor.

When he climbed on top of her, her mouth watered, and her teeth sharpened. Bevon nudged open her legs and pressed his cock to her opening. Without any preamble, he drove into her, sending a rush of endorphins through her that was followed by waves of ecstasy. From there, it only turned better. His kisses thrilled her, his thrusts set her on fire, and his passion took her to new heights.

Zulema ran her hands up and down his back, trying to memorize every inch of his body. When he lowered his lips to her neck, she realized she had no idea what he would do. Since he wasn't a shifter, he wouldn't bite her. She had to be the one. Overwhelmed with need, Zulema followed suit. As if Fate was guiding her, she lowered her lips to that tender spot between his neck and his shoulder blade and sunk her teeth in.

White entombed her, followed by heat of epic proportions. As he kept thrusting into her, her body transcended life itself. Her vision blurred, and then colors of extreme brilliance swam around her. Her own climax built so fast that she couldn't stop the onslaught of pleasure even if she'd tried.

Zulema yelled out her release just as Bevon's cum filled her. The anticipated exhaustion that usually followed didn't happen. Instead, a new energy entered her. It was as if his Fey soul was replacing hers. She just hoped he was experiencing something as close to this.

Time stood still, and her mind failed to understand what was really happening. Zulema just knew that it had been amazing.

When she opened her eyes, it was daylight. How was that possible? She rolled over and found her wonderful mate looking adoringly at her.

"Good morning," he said.

"How is it morning? I'm confused."

He stroked her face. "It will take time for you to adjust to the mating process, but the bottom line was that you became part Fey. I hope you had a good rest, because your body needs it."

"Part Fey?" She had enough powers. Never did she expect to receive anything from him.

"Eventually, you too will be immortal. Can you sweep your hand and clean up the house or whatever you want right now? I don't know."

This was too good to be true. "Do you think you will be able to fly?"

He shook his head. "Kenton never could."

"That doesn't mean you can't. Tory is a pure dragon shifter. I'm part witch, don't forget."

He grinned. "Of that, I am grateful."

While she wanted to spend the day exploring their newfound abilities, they had a killer to take down. "Ugh. For at least a few hours, I forgot about Peter Delaport. That ass."

"Actually, his real name is Penton Tropaled."

"Penton Tropaled? What kind of name is that?"

"Tropaled is Delaport backwards. Personally, I think his new name is better."

"I agree," Zulema said. "What is your master plan?"

"Other than I want my old face back, I'm not sure."

"If you do that, this Penton dude will know I didn't kill you. That won't please him."

Bevon smiled. "That's the plan. He'll just have to do it himself."

"I don't like it."

"He can't kill me," Bevon said. "I doubt he'd use treniam since it would affect him as much."

"Unless he uses gloves."

"There is that."

"Just so you know, I want to help," she said.

Bevon shook his head. "Not going to happen."

He obviously didn't know his new mate all that well yet.

Chapter Twenty-Five

ZULEMA WASN'T COMING with him to confront Penton, and that was that. It was too dangerous. When Bevon pictured going head-to-head against his adversary, regardless of how the battle started, one thing would lead to another, and it would end up a battle of magic.

Zulema might be a witch, but other than her ability to teleport, cloak herself, and use a bit of electricity, her magic wasn't strong enough—at least not yet.

It didn't matter. Bevon was convinced between him and Penton, he was the stronger of the two. The leader of the Zon would eventually back down.

The problem was that after a second humiliating defeat, Penton would eventually send someone after Zulema, and Bevon couldn't have that.

His mate moved closer. "You look like your mind is going a million miles an hour. Care to share?"

"Sure. I can't afford for this vindictive man to ever come after you."

She stiffened. "I can take care of myself."

Ripples of anger entered him, but this time the anger and frustration were coming from Zulema. Bevon could sense when his family was troubled, but he hadn't considered it would happen between him and his mate so soon.

"I have no doubt, princess, especially if you allow me to train you. But training takes time—something we don't have."

"I'm a dragon shifter. Is Penton one?"

"Not that I know of."

"See? I could pick him up, fly high, and drop him to his death."

He did love this woman. "That's great if he doesn't neutralize your powers before you have the chance to use them."

She wagged a finger at him. "I agree, but that's assuming he can see me."

He'd always known she was stubborn. Bevon stroked her cheek. "How about this? The Zon will still be around tomorrow. How about we stick to testing your abilities then—even though you won't be with me during the actual battle? I need to do this by myself."

"Sure. No problem."

He dipped his head. He didn't believe her for a moment. "Zulema. You have no idea what this man is capable of."

She stuck out her chest. "Do you? It's been twenty years. He could have mated with someone and garnered more strength."

He hoped like hell that wasn't true. "I will counter whatever he throws at me."

"Fine, but while I'm seeing what I can do with my newfound powers, how about we see if you can create fire or fly or…"

"Or what? Do you have any secret talents you've been holding back on me?" He failed to hold back a smile.

"I have almost perfect aim when it comes to using a crossbow."

"That was from a lot of practice, I bet."

She blew out a breath. "Possibly."

He stepped closer. "Look, before we make any decisions regarding this upcoming confrontation, we need to go to Feyrion where my mother will release me from this ugly mug. While she is doing that, you catch up with your family. Then we'll see what, if anything you inherited from me."

"Or what you inherited from me."

"That too."

Bevon stroked her cheek and kissed her quick. They dressed and then went outside. He swung his arms in a circle, creating the ring of entry. "Shall we?" he asked.

Together, they stepped through. Once they were on Feyrion, Bevon teleported them to his parents' living room. He telepathed his mother, letting her know she had company.

To his delight, both of his parents arrived. Since Zulema had not met his father, he introduced them. "I am proud to announce that Zulema and I have mated."

His father grinned and then hugged her. "Welcome to the family."

"Thank you, your highness."

His father laughed. "Please call me Leighton."

"Leighton."

His father studied him. "I will never get used to seeing my handsome son look so different."

"It's partially why I'm here. Now that Zulema's family is safe, I would like to be restored to my former self."

His mother smiled. "My pleasure."

"I'll find my family," Zulema telepathed.

His pulse soared. It was so nice not to have to use the bracelets. *"Of course."* He asked his mother where they were.

"Let me show your mate."

"THEY ARE THROUGH that door," Arianna said.

"Thank you."

Bevon's mother disappeared to change Bevon's face back to his original one. Even though everything had gone fairly smoothly in the last few days, Zulema was a bit overwhelmed. Mating with a Fey was still something she hadn't fully believed could happen. The concept she and Bevon could telepath without the bracelet thrilled her, and then being welcomed by his family only added to her joy. The only issue was Bevon insisting on fighting this horrible man by himself.

She knocked on the door that led to a suite of rooms where her sister and mother were staying. When Maylora opened the door, she squealed. "You're back!"

"I am." They hugged.

Aislin stepped up next to Maylora. "How did it go?"

"We need to sit. A lot has happened. Where's Mom?"

"She's outside. She can't get enough of the gardens around here," her sister said.

"I can understand it. I have a lot to tell you—starting with the fact that Bevon and I are now mates."

Excited questions ensued, and Zulema enjoyed regaling them with some of the events that led up to their coupling.

"ALL DONE," HIS mother said. "You are now Bevon Forrester once more. I hope you are ready for a lot of questions about why you put everyone through the trauma of your death."

"I will answer all of their queries as soon as I take care of something."

His mother grabbed his arm. "I can feel your pain. Tell me."

He didn't have time for this. Zulema would be wandering back soon, and he absolutely didn't want her to come with him. This was between him and Penton.

"Remember the man who tried to kill Father about twenty years ago?"

"Of course."

"He's the one who was behind the hit on my life."

His mother sucked in a breath. "I had no idea. You defeated him before, so it should be fine this time—or do I just want to believe that?"

"You have nothing to worry about."

"Remember, you had help last time."

"I recall, but that was because he had a host of men with him. He believes I'm dead. I'll have surprise on my side."

"What about Zulema?" his mother asked.

"I don't want her involved. I couldn't handle it if anything happened to her."

"But she's your mate."

Guilt assaulted him. "I know, but I don't know what, if anything, she inherited from me when we mated. Penton might be able to kill her."

"I see. Be careful," his mother warned.

"I will."

After checking that he had the address that Logan had given Zulema, he teleported outside and then portaled to his cabin. It was no surprise that both Fay and Meena were waiting there—his mother's doing most likely.

"Are you crazy?" Fay said.

"What did Mother say?"

"What do you think?" his other sister answered.

He didn't need his family to hover over him. "I'll be fine. Penton doesn't know I'm alive."

"What are you going to do?" Meena asked. "Just kill him?"

"I wish that were in my nature, but it's not. If he attacks me, however, I will attack back."

His sisters looked at each other. "We can make a weapon for you."

They were sweet. "As a Fey, I have enough weapons."

"Have you seen Penton in the last twenty years? How do you know he hasn't grown in strength?"

They sounded like Zulema. "To really understand his capabilities, I'll have to see for myself. Now if you'll excuse me."

Not needing any help from his sisters, Bevon teleported to the other side of the province. With the address in hand, he was able to find Penton's estate. His home was isolated, which was good. Bevon wanted to make his enemy promise to stay away from him and his family. If he agreed, then Bevon would let him live. Easy, right? It would be if he could trust the ass to keep his word.

Since Bevon's magic often required space, he teleported to the back of the home, keeping himself cloaked. He wouldn't be surprised if Penton had a few bodyguards around the premises.

When Bevon arrived, he spotted his nemesis. Just because no one else was around, it didn't mean they were alone.

Bevon uncloaked himself. "Oh, Penton. May I have a word?"

His adversary spun around. His jaw dropped, and his face paled. Perfect. "You're d…dead!"

That confirmed that Penton had been the one to order the hit on him. "Clearly, you're mistaken. Hard to kill a Fey, remember?"

"I knew it was too good to be true when Valoric claimed to have succeeded. But as they always say, if you want the job done right, you have to do it yourself."

Without any warning, the man raised his arms and sent out a powerful blast in Bevon's direction that was so strong, it knocked him on his ass. What the hell? Sure, he believed Penton had powers, but his seemed to have grown over the years.

Bevon dusted off his pride and stood. He could have cloaked himself, but where was the nobility in that? Using his talent to move things at will, he returned a forceful blast at Penton. The man tumbled backward and likewise landed on his butt. *Take that, asshole.*

This back and forth was merely a preamble to the real fight. Bevon expected the rest of Penton's warriors to show up en masse, but no one came.

"Why did you want me dead so badly?" Bevon asked as Penton rose to his feet and brushed the dirt off his arms and butt. "Waiting twenty years seems excessive to hold a grudge."

"You don't know?"

If he knew, he wouldn't need to ask. "No. Enlighten me."

"I wanted you dead so that Kenton would come after me to exact his revenge."

This was all about killing Kenton? It actually made sense. If both of the Forrester sons were dead, their father might be easier to remove from power. "Why not take out Kenton first?"

"He has that dragon shifter for a mate."

Interesting, but so do I. Only he'd insisted that Zulema remain back on Feyrion. "That's true. I guess it's you and me."

"I am looking forward to it." One minute, Penton was a man, and the next he'd grown into a fifteen-foot tall dragon.

Well, shit. How the hell had that happened? Zulema had been right. He must have mated with a dragon. Then again, so had Bevon. Too bad Feys rarely took on the characteristics of their mate.

But I'm a witch, too, Zulema had said.

Penton's dragon shot a stream of fire that headed straight toward Bevon, taking him by surprise. He immediately held out both palms to deflect the flames. As soon as the heat reached him, Bevon thrust a force field at it to keep it at bay. While he could have created a protective dome around himself to stop any further assault, that wouldn't give him any kind of advantage. Besides, hiding was not his style.

Penton roared, acting like he truly believed he was superior. As if his adversary's indignation was the needed catalyst, Bevon's bones cracked and pain shot through him as his body grew. And grew. And grew. He'd never been shocked by anything—until now. The ground fell beneath him, and his skin stretched and morphed. What the hell? When he looked at his arms, they'd transformed into wings. Holy shit. He'd shifted. Bevon wasn't certain how that was even possible, but he was glad it had.

His enemy charged toward him. If Bevon didn't get the hell out of the way now, Penton could seriously injure him. While he still believed he was immortal, it's possible that was true only if he was in his human form.

Move! said some internal voice.

Bevon flapped his wings hard and fast, causing him to soar upward. His shot of joy at his achievement was short-lived. While Bevon would have loved to bask in the glory of this new form, he couldn't afford to. Penton was coming at him with his long claws extended.

Since arriving on Tarradon, Bevon had watched many dragon

fights, but for the life of him, he couldn't think of what to do to take down Penton. Going on the offense seemed the best defense. His brother had mentioned many times what an amazing fighter Tory was. If he recalled, all one needed to do to kill a dragon was pierce the spot below the heart and tug. The maneuver might sound easy, but he had no idea how to achieve it. His wings were bulky. If he collided with Penton, no telling what might happen.

Before he could make up his mind what to do, Penton drove toward him. All Bevon could think of was to change the air current around his adversary to throw him off balance, but when Bevon tried, his magic didn't seem to be working. Damn.

Dragons couldn't laugh, but he swore Penton was smiling or rather gloating at going up against a novice. Bevon would show him. It was now or never. Like he'd seen other dragons do, he dove under Penton with the purpose of flipping over and clawing at the man's underbelly.

It was a brilliant tactic, except that when he tried to change position, he didn't have the agility to turn over. Claws dug into his wing, causing an ache so strong, Bevon lost the ability to lift one wing. Oh, shit. He was going down.

Chapter Twenty-Six

A JOLT OF pain shot through Zulema so hard, it knocked the breath out of her.

Maylora rushed up to her. "What happened?"

"I don't know. I've never felt anything like that before in my life. Crap."

"Come sit down," her sister said.

Only then did she remember that Bevon had told her that when they mated, she'd be able to feel any extreme emotion—like love or pain—that came from him.

"No. It's Bevon. He's in trouble." And here, she thought he was downstairs.

Zulema teleported to the living room, but it was empty. *"Arianna?"* she telepathed.

His mother immediately appeared. "What is it?"

"It's Bevon. I think he is hurt. Do you know where he is?"

"He is with Penton Tropaled."

"Why didn't he tell me?"

Arianna placed a hand on Zulema's arm. "He didn't want to take any chances that you might be injured."

"I appreciate his concern, but now he's hurt."

Not wanting his mother to stop her from going to him, she teleported outside. She had no idea if she could create a portal by herself, but it didn't matter. She still had the medallion that Derrick had given her. With a few wide sweeps, she portaled to Bevon's cabin on Tarradon. Even though she'd memorized Penton's address, she wasn't certain where it was.

As if Fay could sense her presence, his sister appeared. "Thank goddess, you're here," Zulema said.

"I sensed it too. Bevon is hurt."

"I know."

"Do you know where Penton is?" Fay asked.

"Yes. I have the address." She rattled it off.

"Directions aren't my specialty, but I think I can find it. Hang on," Fay said.

When they arrived, screeches and cries filled the air, and Zulema's heart nearly burst. "Thank you. I'll take it from here."

"I'll be standing by should you need me," Fay said.

"Thank you."

While Zulema couldn't be positive which dragon was Bevon and which one was Penton, the fact one had some purple scales and was injured, implied that was Bevon.

"Hold on. I'm here," she told him.

"I can do this," he shot back, sounding rather angry and yet determined.

Not with an injured wing he couldn't. Zulema totally understood that his ego would be damaged if she came to the rescue, but no dragon with a broken wing would stand a chance against an experienced fighter.

To hell with it. She shifted and soared upward, ready to take down this bastard. Right before she attacked, Penton clamped down hard on Bevon's tail, rendering his ability to maneuver fairly useless. His pain, coupled with the horror of watching him suffer, caused a momentary lapse in her focus.

Bevon flapped his one good wing, but it wasn't enough to keep him afloat. Had he been more experienced, he would have been able to last a bit longer. He dropped like a stone and crashed to the ground.

"Are you okay?" she telepathed. It was probably stupid to ask, but Zulema had to make certain he was still alive.

To her dismay, Bevon didn't answer. In fact, no reaction registered, but she refused to believe he was dead. Bevon Forrester was immortal—or at least he claimed to be when in his human form. If Bevon had died, Fay would have felt it—as would Kenton, she bet. His brother and mate would be here in a flash.

Penton came after her, jarring her out of her despair. *Big mistake, buddy.* Zulema had spent her life training to fight, and with her adrenaline surging through her body, this murderer was going down.

It was possible she'd inherited some of Bevon's Fey powers, but now wasn't the time to test any theories. She went with general tactics. Zulema executed a dive. Penton followed, just as she'd hoped. Before she crashed into the ground, Zulema swooped upward so fast he didn't have time to change direction before their bodies met. Only she was prepared for the impact. Digging her nails into his gut, she ripped her talons downward as hard as she could. His screech of pain encouraged her to attack again. And again.

Despite her strong hold, he managed to get away before she could stab him right below his heart. Before he took off, he managed to twist around and punctured her wing, but the damage was minimal.

She looked to the ground to see if Bevon had moved. Yes! He'd shifted back, but his body appeared broken.

In order to take down Penton, she had to injure him further. She soared above him, and then shot downward as fast as she could. It was always possible he'd turn over and attack, but it was a chance she had to take. Her speed seemed faster than she ever remembered, and she reached him in a second. With her claws extended, she gouged out one of his eyes. He'd eventually heal—assuming he lived that long—but for now he was in pain and partially blind.

As if he was willing to admit defeat, he flew to the ground, landed with a thud, and shifted. It was time for her to end this.

She landed next to Bevon and shifted back. When she shot electricity from her arms toward this murderer, Penton staggered, but it didn't do as much damage as she'd hoped. She needed Bevon to help.

With seemingly great effort, he rose, but was only able to stand on one leg. The other leg appeared to be broken. While waves of pain were running through her, anger was added to the mix. "Let's get him," Bevon growled.

"You can't go after him in your condition," she telepathed.

"I don't intend to." With a sweep of a hand, he created a puddle under Penton. Immediately, she understood the tactic. Zulema shot out another bolt of power, but it didn't create the desired lethal effect. "Help me," she said to Bevon. "We need to join forces."

She couldn't be sure if he possessed the power of electricity, but if he could transform into a dragon, she bet he could harness this ability. Zulema grabbed hold of his arm and squeezed. "Think about sending this ass to his death by generating a charge so great, he'll crumble."

Concentrating with all of her might, she forced out the largest electric bolt she'd ever created, but all that did was knock Penton down. What was it going to take?

"I got this," Bevon said. As if he was willing to use all of his reserve energy, he manifested a charge so strong, it turned Penton Tropaled to dust. The sizzle of burning flesh sickened her, but she wasn't sorry to see him go.

"Nice job, mate."

Bevon grinned and then winced.

Just when she was about to rejoice and suggest they leave, two other men came at them with guns in hand. She only had seconds to react. "I need a crossbow," she mostly said to herself.

Zulema had no idea if Bevon could create one, but if he could make a whole meal in seconds, he certainly should be able to do this. One second, her hands were empty, and the next, she had her crossbow with the arrow in place ready to go, and then one appeared in his hands.

"Got mine, too," he announced with pride. "Only I don't know how to use it."

They didn't have time for a lesson. Penton's guards would be on them in another two seconds. "Keeping your fingers under the rail, take aim and trust that you inherited my perfect aim."

They both looked through the scope, and at the same time, pulled the trigger. The men's guns fired, but the two arrows hit the men a split second before. The attackers dropped to the ground, and the bullets went wide.

She stood there in shock.

"Zulema, we need to go."

"How? You can't walk."

Fay appeared next to them. "I'll create a portal," she said.

Seconds later, they were in a bedroom at Bevon's parents' castle. She and Fay placed him on the bed, but he waved a hand. "I'll be fine."

"From the way your leg is at a rather odd angle, I'd say you broke it. Rest," Zulema said. "Your inner dragon should heal you by morning."

"Or Fay can help."

She planted a hand on her hip. "Is that all I am to you? Your savior and guardian angel?"

He laughed. "You are so much more than that, though I'm afraid I'd have to give Zulema the title of savior today."

"I can't take all the credit. In all honesty, you weakened Penton—assuming he was the dragon. Even after I drove him to the ground, I couldn't stop him with my electricity. You provided the fatal charge."

Bevon brushed his chest with his knuckles in that odd motion again. "I guess you are right."

His mother rushed in. "Okay, everyone out, please—except for Fay. I could use your help. I'll need a few minutes with my son, though I am tempted to let him suffer a little longer. He should know better than to go off on his own to fight an unknown enemy."

"He's dead, Mother. At least Penton won't be coming after us."

"No, but the rest of the clan might."

Zulema had worried about that. She left to find Maylora, her mom, and Aislin. It was time for them to return to Tarradon. Zulema could take them back herself, but she had the sense Bevon wanted to talk to them first. He would ask them to keep what they learned quiet.

Zulema knocked on the room where her sister and Aislin were staying. When the door opened, she was warmly welcomed. "Where did you go?" her sister asked.

"It's a long story. Is Mom still outside?"

"No, she's in her room."

"I can get her," Aislin offered.

That would be great. Zulema wasn't up for telling the story twice.

BEVON SWUNG HIS legs over the bed, tested that he was healed, and stood. "As always, thank you."

His mother shook her head. "You have to stop playing hero."

"I'll try. Now that Zulema and her family are safe, I'm hoping my life returns to normal."

His mom chuckled. "I bet living with Zulema will be anything but normal."

At one time, he thought he'd never settle down, mostly because he liked the challenge of meeting new people—women in particular. Only after meeting his mate did he realize how empty his life had been. "You are very right."

"Her family will be returning to Tarradon," his mother said.

He understood that tone. "Should I erase the memory of all three? If I do, it will make it harder on Zulema to talk with them."

"I understand. How about letting her mother and sister know about us, but not the friend?"

"My thoughts exactly."

His mother hugged him. "Please don't be such a stranger."

Her warmth and love were welcome. "I won't. I promise."

Instead of teleporting, he opted to walk back down to the parlor. *"Zulema, it's time for us and your family to return to Tarradon. Can we speak for a moment?"*

She appeared next to him in a flash. "Are we alone?" she asked with lust clouding her eyes.

"We are, but we should really wait until we get back to Tarradon."

"Why Bevon Forrester, do you always have sex on your mind?"

He laughed. It was the same line he'd told her when they were on top of a mountain. "Usually, but this time I was merely asking if we could talk in private."

Uh-huh. "What did you want to ask me? I'm guessing it's about letting my family know about Feyrion."

"It is. I've spoken with my mother. We feel you need to be able to speak freely with your sister and mother about your life with me."

"But not Aislin."

"No."

She nodded. "I understand. You mentioned that Kenton had erased Tory's memory after she came here to recover."

"Yes."

"Will it hurt?" Zulema asked.

"No."

"Okay. I'll tell them to get ready."

Zulema left, and Bevon dropped down onto the sofa. He thought that once this whole affair with Derrick—or rather Penton—wanting him dead had passed, that life would be simple. Unfortunately, he could see that might not be the case.

Someone knocked on the front door, and a moment later, Tamarella's mother and father rushed in. "Oh, my goodness. It's true. You're alive. How is that possible?"

He stood and hugged both of them. They deserved to know what role their daughter played in all of this. "I had to have some very bad people believe I was dead. In the end, that person was brought to justice. Please have a seat. I'm afraid Tam was caught in the middle and paid the price."

For the next few minutes, he told them of the evil plan to take down his father. He explained that Tamarella was killed in order to make Derrick exact revenge. Penton let Derrick believe that Bevon was the killer. "If someone had succeeded in killing me, then Kenton would have gone after Penton. A trap would have been set."

"With both of you out of the way, Penton might have succeeded in overthrowing your father," Tam's father said.

"Exactly. The whole thing sickens me. I am so sorry that your family got tangled up in this mess."

"It's not your fault. Derrick Valoric was not a good man, but we both believe he loved our daughter," Aunt Drina said.

"He did, and it cost him his life too. Please let Tristan know that his letter was intercepted and changed. The man who hurt William has not been caught, yet, but I will see to it that he is."

"Thank you, Bevon. We appreciate all that you've done. I'm sure much of Feyrion will be happy to learn you are alive."

"I imagine my mother will tell them all."

Zulema came downstairs with her mother, sister, and Aislin in tow.

"Anna?" his aunt asked.

Bevon stood. "No. That was another part of the ruse. This is Zulema Garcia, my mate. She had to pretend to be Tam's friend in order to gather information about her death."

"I see," Aunt Drina said. She held out her hand. "Nice to meet you."

Bevon moved over to his mate. "We need to be going. Again, I am sorry."

"Thank you."

Once they walked outside, he created a portal. He swore Zulema's mother's eyes grew wider than any platter in the castle's pantry.

"Ladies?"

Seconds later, they were on Tarradon in the woods. He faced Zulema. "Why don't you escort your sister and mother home, and

I'll take Aislin back to her house?"

She wrung her hands together. "What am I going to tell my boss about why I was gone for so long?"

She certainly couldn't tell the truth, especially since he planned to erase her memory. "Let's get you home, and I'll help you come up with a story."

Aislin hugged Zulema and Maylora goodbye. "I'm glad everything worked out for you," her friend said.

"Me, too."

As soon as Zulema teleported her family home, he touched Aislin's arm and teleported her to her home. "Before I leave, there is something I need to do," he told her.

"What's that?"

She wouldn't remember afterward, so there was no harm in telling her about his plan to erase her memory. "I can't have you tell anyone about Feyrion."

"I promise, I won't."

"People have ways of extracting the information."

She glanced to the floor. "Like kidnapping me again?"

"Yes, which is why I need to erase your memory. It will only take a moment and won't hurt."

"Do I have a choice?"

He liked her feisty attitude. "Not really."

"Okay, go ahead."

Bevon placed his fingertips on her temples and focused his attention on her memories. Within seconds, they were gone.

He stepped back and held up his hands. "I'm Zulema's mate, and you've had an accident."

"What?"

"Apparently, you were outside, and someone hit you over the head. Don't you remember?"

Yes, it was a bit cruel not to tell her anything about what really occurred, but it was necessary.

"No, but where's Zulema?"

"She's with her sister. I'm about to meet her now."

Aislin touched the back of her head. "I don't even feel a bump."

"That's why I'm here. I healed you."

Her mouth opened. "You're a healer. Thank you."

He inhaled. "If you're okay, I need to get back to Zulema."

"Of course and thank you."

Deception was never easy, but in this case, it was for her welfare. He teleported back to his cabin, ready to start his life with his new mate.

Chapter Twenty-Seven

Z ULEMA HAD NEVER been happier. Though why she agreed to join Bevon in his training with Tory's brother Thane she didn't know. The man was relentless. He put them through obstacle courses, mat work, and general fitness drills. Bevon looked as if it required no energy on his part, but Zulema was at her limit.

"Can we take a break?" she asked.

"Come on, princess. We are getting really good at this teamwork stuff."

She had to admit that doing battle with a partner was something she'd never considered before. "That's true."

Her cell rang.

"Answer it," Thane said. "I can tell you want to."

"I'll only be a minute."

She rushed over to her phone. When she saw the caller ID, her stomach tightened. It was her former boss—the one who found bodyguard jobs for her. She and Bevon had discussed what she was going to do with her life. Money was no longer an issue since he had plenty for ten life times, but she missed the work.

"Hello?"

"Well, well, I thought you'd been kidnapped or something."

That was funny. She hadn't mentioned anything to her boss about her job to kill Bevon, nor about mating with him. "Just took a break for a bit, but I'm back now."

"I have a job for you."

Excitement charged through her, but then the reality kicked in. "How long is it for?"

"Just three days."

"Days, nights, or both?"

"You can have days if you want. Is there something you're not telling me?" Her female boss was quite intuitive.

"I have found my mate, and I want to spend as much time with him as possible."

"That's wonderful, but you still want to work, right?"

"Yes, but less frequently," Zulema said.

He understood that she might miss having her own career and encouraged to take a few jobs here and there. Besides, there would be times when he had to do Feyrion business, too.

"I can make that work," her boss said.

When she hung up, Zulema couldn't help but smile. Bevon came over to her. "I can see you're happy. Tell me all about it."

"I agreed to do a small job. Three days max—and only during the day."

"That's great."

"Thank you. Before I go back to work, I thought we could take a little trip." She'd found this delightful little lake. While it wasn't as spectacular as the one she'd seen on Feyrion, this one was deep, and Bevon could benefit from learning how to swim in his dragon form.

"I'm game." He turned back to Thane. "We're going to go. Zulema has something planned for us."

"No problem. Next week, the guardians are doing some mock battles, assuming you two want to join in. I'll warn you it will be quite competitive."

"If Finn is there, I'm in too."

"Oh, he'll be there for sure."

"Then you can count on us," Bevon said.

Once they stepped outside, Zulema faced him. "I thought it might be fun to go for a little swim. Afterward, who knows?"

He grinned. "You are a temptress."

"We'll see. Ready?"

"Always."

They stepped away from each other and shifted. Seeing Bevon in his dragon form never failed to excite her. She soared upward, and Bevon followed.

"Where are we going, exactly?" he telepathed.

"You'll see."

He flew next to her for the half hour trip. The scenery wasn't as richly intense as that on Feyrion, but it was still beautiful. When she spotted the water, she dove straight for it. Bevon would assume they'd land on the beach, strip, and swim, but that wasn't what she had in mind.

As she neared the surface, she tucked in her wings and dove straight in. The liquid cooled her heated body.

"Can dragons swim?" Bevon telepathed.

"I hope so." Of course, she was kidding. *"Use your tail for propulsion."*

A huge splash rippled the water next to her. Ouch. Bevon's wings weren't tucked in as close to his body as they should have been, but he'd figure it out in a moment. Because she was in a sassy mood, Zulema circled him, loving the freedom of the water. Being able to hold her breath for a long time was an added bonus.

"This is fun," he relayed.

Bevon caught on so fast that soon he was swimming around her. Wanting a bit more of Bevon, Zulema shot out of the water and zoomed upward. Once she was mostly dry, she found a perfect spot on the sand to land.

A moment later, Bevon was beside her. Because they were alone, she thought this would be a good place to enjoy each other. "How about creating a dome around us for privacy?" she asked.

He shifted. "Why don't you try it?"

Zulema had tried a few things, but her abilities were sporadic. They both hoped that with time, she would be as powerful as him. "Do I just sweep my hand in an arc and mentally picture the bubble?"

"It's a bit more complicated. I'll do it this time, but only because

I want you too much."

"I like the sound of that."

Once the bubble was in place, she quickly divested him of his clothes using her newfound magic.

"My turn." He swept a hand, and a moment later, she was naked. "I like it. I can't imagine how talented our children are going to be."

Her pulse skyrocketed. While she'd quickly agreed to moving into his cabin in the woods, they hadn't discussed much else. "Our children? How many are you planning on?"

He shrugged. "Ten or twenty should suffice."

A laugh burst out. "With just me? Or are you going to hire a gaggle of women to help produce and raise them all?"

He swept a hand and created a large blanket on the beach. "Perhaps I was a bit overambitious. What do you say we try for just one first?"

"Now?"

"Absolutely."

Life with Bevon Forrester was going to be one adventure after another.

I hope you enjoyed reading Zulema and Bevon's story as much as I enjoyed writing it.

Don't forget to sign up for my newsletter *to receive a free book, as well as up-to-date information on my stories. If you prefer to only receive notices regarding my releases, follow me on BookBub.*

http://smarturl.it/VellaDayNL

bookbub.com/authors/vella-day

THE END

A WITCH'S COVE MYSTERY (Paranormal Cozy Mystery)
PINK Is The New Black (book 1)
A PINK Potion Gone Wrong (book 2)
The Mystery of the PINK Aura (book 3)
Box Set (books 1-3)
Sleuthing In The PINK (book 4)
Not in The PINK (book 5)
Gone in the PINK of an Eye (book 6)

HIDDEN REALMS OF SILVER LAKE (Paranormal Romance)
Awakened By Flames (book 1)
Seduced By Flames (book 2)
Kissed By Flames (book 3)
Destiny In Flames (book 4)
Box Set (books 1-4)
Passionate Flames (book 5)
Ignited By Flames (book 6)
Touched By Flames (book 7)
Box Set (books 5-7)
Bound By Flames (book 8)
Fueled By Flames (book 9)
Scorched By Flames (book 10)

FOUR SISTERS OF FATE: HIDDEN REALMS OF SILVER LAKE (Paranormal Romance)
Poppy (book 1)
Primrose (book 2)
Acacia (book 3)
Magnolia (book 4)
Box Set (books 1-4)
Jace (book 5)
Tanner (book 6)

WERES AND WITCHES OF SILVER LAKE (Paranormal Romance)

A Magical Shift (book 1)
Catching Her Bear (book 2)
Surge of Magic (book 3)
The Bear's Forbidden Wolf (book 4)
Her Reluctant Bear (book 5)
Freeing His Tiger (book 6)
Protecting His Wolf (book 7)
Waking His Bear (book 8)
Melting Her Wolf's Heart (book 9)
Her Wolf's Guarded Heart (book 10)
His Rogue Bear (book 11)
Box Set (books 1-4)
Box Set (books 5-8)
Reawakening Their Bears (book 12)

PACK WARS (Paranormal Romance)
Training Their Mate (book 1)
Claiming Their Mate (book 2)
Rescuing Their Virgin Mate (book 3)
Box Set (books 1-3)
Loving Their Vixen Mate (book 4)
Fighting For Their Mate (book 5)
Enticing Their Mate (book 6)
Box Set (books 1-4)
Complete Box Set (books 1-6)

HIDDEN HILLS SHIFTERS (Paranormal Romance)
An Unexpected Diversion (book 1)
Bare Instincts (book 2)
Shifting Destinies (book 3)
Embracing Fate (book 4)
Promises Unbroken (book 5)
Bare 'N Dirty (book 6)
Hidden Hills Shifters Complete Box Set (books 1-6)

MONTANA PROMISES (Full length contemporary Romance)
Promises of Mercy (book 1)
Foundations For Three (book 2)
Montana Fire (book 3)
Montana Promises Box Set (books 1-3)
Hart To Hart (Book 4)
Burning Seduction (Book 5)
Montana Promises Complete Box Set (books 1-5)

ROCK HARD, MONTANA (contemporary romance novellas)
Montana Desire (book 1)
Awakening Passions (book 2)

PLEDGED TO PROTECT (contemporary romantic suspense)
From Panic To Passion (book 1)
From Danger To Desire (book 2)
From Terror To Temptation (book 3)
Pledged To Protect Box Set (books 1-3)

BURIED SERIES (contemporary romantic suspense)
Buried Alive (book 1)
Buried Secrets (book 2)
Buried Deep (book 3)
The Buried Series Complete Box Set (books 1-3)

A NASH MYSTERY (Contemporary Romance)
Sidearms and Silk(book 1)
Black Ops and Lingerie(book 2)
A Nash Mystery Box Set (books 1-2)

STARTER SETS (Romance)
Contemporary
Paranormal

Author Bio

Love it HOT and STEAMY? Sign up for my newsletter and receive MONTANA DESIRE for FREE. smarturl.it/o4cz93?IQid=MLite

OR Are you a fan of quirky PARANORMAL COZY MYSTERIES? Sign up for this newsletter. smarturl.it/CozyNL

Not only do I love to read, write, and dream, I'm an extrovert. I enjoy being around people and am always trying to understand what makes them tick. Not only must my romance books have a happily ever after, I need characters I can relate to. My men are wonderful, dynamic, smart, strong, and the best lovers in the world (of course).

My Paranormal Cozy Mysteries are where I let my imagination run wild with witches and a talking pink iguana who believes he's a real sleuth.

I believe I am the luckiest woman. I do what I love and I have a wonderful, supportive husband, who happens to be hot!

Fun facts about me

(1) I'm a math nerd who loves spreadsheets. Give me numbers and I'll find a pattern.

(2) I live on a Costa Rica beach!

(3) I also like to exercise. Yes, I know I'm odd.

I love hearing from readers either on FB or via email (hint, hint).

Social Media Sites

Website:
www.velladay.com

FB:
facebook.com/vella.day.90

Twitter:
@velladay4

Gmail:
velladayauthor@gmail.com